THE
LAUREL AND HARDY
MURDERS

Mysteries From Wildside Press

Earl Derr Biggers

The Agony Column
Fifty Candles

Michael Bracken

Bad Girls: One Dozen Dangerous Dames
Deadly Campaign
Tequila Sunrise

David Dvorkin

The Cavaradossi Killings
Time for Sherlock Holmes

Joe L. Hensley

Robak's Cross
Robak's Fire
Robak's Firm
A Killing in Gold
The Poison Summer
Song of Corpus Juris
Final Doors
Rivertown Risk
Outcasts

Marvin Kaye

My Brother the Druggist
My Son the Druggist
A Lively Game of Murder
The Soap Opera Slaughters
Bullets for Macbeth
The Country Music Murders

Ray Faraday Nelson

Dog-Headed Death

Hayford Peirce

Trouble in Tahiti: Blood on the Hibiscus
Trouble in Tahiti: Commissaire Tama, Chief of Police
Trouble in Tahiti: P.I. Joe Caneili, Discrétion Assurée

THE
LAUREL AND HARDY
MURDERS

MARVIN KAYE

A WILDSIDE PRESS MYSTERY

THE LAUREL AND HARDY MURDERS

Published by:

Wildside Press
P.O. Box 45
Gillette, NJ 07933-0045
www.wildsidepress.com

First Wildside Press Edition:
June 2001

10 9 8 7 6 5 4 3 2 1

To Dave Ossar
for introducing me to the Old Man
and allowing me to give him a home

IN LIEU OF ACKNOWLEDGMENTS

It would ill befit the demi-callipygian spirit of the Sons of the Desert to begin with a dry set of formal acknowledgments. Instead, I propose a round of toasts:

To Exhausted Ruler Jack McCabe for permission to reprint the SOTD constitution, and for tons of data in his excellent books;

To Grand Sheik Al Kilgore; past parent tent president Dwain Smith; Al Barbour, and the other New York officers and committee members (all 812) for permission to reprint excerpts from the By-Laws; and also to Al Kilgore for a few gags;

To past president Tye Morrow for friendship and leadership;
To Dick Baldwin, for contributing gags, especially for the committee meeting sequence;

To Jim Dukas and Dick Baldwin again for working up with me the formula for the initiation ceremony;

To His Excellency Sir Barry Alan Richmond (a more complete panoply of titles appears elsewhere), for being a good sport, for gags, and for one very special, confidential favor;

To Roger Gordon, president of the Two Tars and editor of *The Intertent Journal*, for support in its pages; my apologies for providing an impossible bad evening for the Philadelphia Sons, not to mention a VP whom they'd have better sense than to elect;

To Tom Dillon, Shepherd of The Lambs, in memory of a beloved home, here resurrected anachronistically with minor architectural modifications;

To Marty Kondak, Poet Lariat of the Sons of the Desert, for the form if not the contents of certain included toasts;

To Alex Soma for bringing me a bag of hard-boiled eggs and nuts when it hurt to laugh.

But especially:

TO BEN and LUCILLE HARDY PRICE and IDA LAUREL with warm memories of gracious meetings at SOTD banquets,

and

TO MAE BUSCH and CHARLEY HALL who are eternally ever-popular,

TO FIN

TO BABE

AND to STAN, all of whom are eternally with us.

Hear, hear!

FIRST REEL: *8mm silent.*

Mr. Butler and Mr. Poe always saw eye to
eye. Neither would turn his back on the
other.

When Wayne Poe dropped dead during the June banquet show at The Lambs, most members of the Sons of the Desert agreed it was the first really funny thing he ever did onstage. But I knew differently. In Philadelphia, a few weeks earlier, the comic received a standing ovation from a roomful of people who hated his guts.

Why was Poe so unpopular? Hal Fawkes or Natie Barrows or Dutchy Hovis would give three different answers based on personal enmity, and Frank Butler (an S.O.B. in his own right) would naturally contribute an ear-blistering paragraph or two of particulars. But the real reason no one could stand Poe was best expressed by the venerable trouper Jack Black, of the old vaudeville team of Black and White.

It was the afternoon of the June banquet. O. J. and I picked Black up at the upstate home for retired AGVA artists. He was our guest of honor, and fortunately the weather was mild enough to permit him to venture forth. He was, after all, well past ninety. During the ride, Black took O. J. to task for permitting Poe to appear on the evening's program. "Smith and Dale. Laurel and Hardy. Bobby Clark. Chaplin. Harold Lloyd. Langdon. Keaton." The nonagenarian's thin, sharp, cracked voice continued for nearly a minute cataloging the comedy greats of half a century. "And you have the nerve to include Wayne Poe?" he challenged O. J., who smiled his eternally diffident grin. "Producing laughter is an art. Poe is a disgrace to that tradition!"

It wasn't because Poe was incapable of making people laugh. Some of his pirated punch lines—stolen from new comics he heard at the Improv, Catch a Rising Star, the Champagne Cellar, and other showcase clubs—were funny enough to

3

garner guffaws if pronounced by a computer. But Poe's delivery was lousy, his timing was dreadful, and he indulged in slapstick without having the technique to bring it off. He never knew when to get offstage, so no matter what audience response he started with, it eventually slid downhill. When the inevitable slump set in, he would shift to the desperate comic's terminal ploy, insult humor.

On top of everything else, Poe thought he was a born singer, and sometimes prolonged his already overlong turns with uninspired musical interludes which at least had the virtue of being marginally better than his undisciplined assays at shtick.

Finally, and perhaps worst of all, Wayne Poe was an incurable punster. I say "perhaps" because the point is arguable. Hilary, who likes plays on words, holds that the pun is a form of cerebration distantly related to logic problems and acrostic puzzles. Personally, I regard incessant punning as excellent grounds for excusable homicide.

At any rate, all of Poe's doubtful professional accomplishments were mine to witness firsthand in Philadelphia, at the annual banquet of the Two Tars.

"Who in hell are the Sons of the Desert?" Hilary Quayle asked without looking up. Her eyes were glued to a press release about Brian Lucas, the singer, which her fingers were swiftly constructing in the carriage of her Adler automatic. "And since when," she added, "do you support the U.A.R.?"

"Not guilty," I said, placing my membership card to the parent tent (or founding chapter) of the Sons under her pert nose so she could see the picture of Stan and Ollie. "We're an organization devoted to Laurel and Hardy films and, by extension, the furtherance of the comedic art."

She nodded. "No wonder you're a member."

I ignored it. "Sons of the Desert is the name of one of the best of the Laurel and Hardy feature films."

She turned the card over and examined the escutcheon designed for the society by Al Kilgore. It consisted of a lion and a unicorn, smugly and sleepily resting against the crown that the mythic beasties were reputed to prize enough to fight over. Beneath the golden round, a buckled oval housed and bore, respectively, the immortal neck- and headwear of Laurel and Hardy: a bowtie for Stan, a cravat capable of being twiddled for Ollie, and two bowlers, one thin, the other fat. Comedy and tragedy masks resembling the boys' faces, and a Latin legend completed the shield.

"What does this mean?" Hilary inquired, her finger tapping the inscription. "Duae tabulae rasae in quibus nihil scriptum est."

I could have commented on her lack of a classical education, but I was studiously avoiding repartee. "Literally," I replied, "it means something like 'Two slates on which nothing has been written.' It's a proximate translation of the motto Stan himself suggested for the club.''

"Which is?''

Holding up a hand for a moment's patience, I went to my room and fished out the copy of the SOTD by-laws. I opened the booklet to page two and waited while she read it.

Constitution of The Sons of the Desert
by John McCabe, Exhausted Ruler

Article I. The Sons of the Desert is an organization with scholarly overtones and heavily social undertones devoted to the loving study of the persons and films of Stan Laurel and Oliver Hardy.

Article II. The founding members are Orson Bean, Al Kilgore, John McCabe, Chuck McCann and John Municino.

Article III. The Sons of the Desert shall have the following officers and board members who will be elected at an annual meeting:

Grand Sheik

Vice-Sheik
(Sheik in charge of vice)

Grand Vizier
(Corresponding Secretary)

Sub-Vice-Vizier
(Treasurer
and in charge of sub-vice)

Board Members-at-Large
(This number shall not
exceed 812)

Article IV. All officers and members of the Board shall sit at an exalted place at the annual banquet table.

Article V. The officers and members of the Board shall have absolutely no authority whatever.

Article VI. Despite his absolute lack of authority, the Grand Sheik or his deputy shall act as chairman at all meetings, and will follow the standard parliamentary procedure in conducting same. At the meetings, it is hoped that the innate dignity, sensitivity, and good taste of the members assembled will permit activities to be conducted with a lively sense of deportment and good order.

Article VII. Article 6 is ridiculous.

Article VIII. The Annual Meeting shall be conducted in the following sequence:
  a. Cocktails.
  b. Business meeting and cocktails.
  c. Dinner (with cocktails).
  d. After-dinner speeches and cocktails.
  e. Cocktails.
  f. Coffee and cocktails.
  g. Showing of Laurel and Hardy film.
  h. After-film critique and cocktails.
  i. After-after-film critique and cocktails.
  j. Stan has suggested this period. In his words: "All members are requested to park their camels and hire a taxi; then return for 'One for the desert'!"

Article IX. Section "d" above shall consist in part of the following toasts:

  1—"To Stan"
  2—"To Babe"
  3—"To Fin"
  4—"To Mae Busch and Charley Hall—who are eternally ever-popular."

Article X. Section "h" above shall include the reading of scholarly papers on Laurel and Hardy. Any member going over an 8½-minute time limit will have his cocktails limited to fourteen in number.

Article XI. Hopefully, and seriously, The Sons of the Desert, in the strong desire to perpetuate the spirit and genius of Laurel and Hardy will conduct activities ultimately and always devoted to the preservation of their films and the encouragement of their showing everywhere.

Article XII. There shall be member societies in other cities called "Tents," each of which shall derive its name from one of the films.

Article XIII. Stan has suggested that members might wear a fez or blazer patch with an appropriate motto. He says: "I hope that the motto can be blue and gray, showing two derbies with these words superimposed: 'Two minds without a single thought.' ''

These words have been duly set into the delightful escutcheon created for The Sons of the Desert by Al Kilgore. They have been rendered into Latin in the spirit of Stan's dictum that our organization should have, to use his words, ''a half-assed dignity'' about it.

We shall strive to maintain precisely that kind of dignity at all costs—at all times.

By the time she finished it, Hilary had a crease at one side of her mouth, her self-conscious version of a grin. I was glad to see it. Lately, we'd been snipping at one another because of the phone-call argument, but since I now had a favor to ask, it behooved me to establish a lighter atmosphere.

The phone-call quarrel was an offshoot of the anxiety Hilary started to feel between April 15 and the mid-year estimated assessment. First, she began to grumble about being tax-poor, then went on an economy kick. Finally, she accused me of running up her phone bill by making too many outside calls to other women. This was absolutely untrue. A few times, I *received* calls from Pat Lowe and Penny Saxon, but Hilary wouldn't believe they were incoming. Yet I've told her repeatedly that the only times I use the office telephone for personal reasons are when I want to fix my fast-running wrist-watch or check on the weather conditions on Westside Highway.

Of course, I'm well aware that the phone hassle is really symptomatic of deeper trouble between us. First, Hilary is not only jealous, but percipient enough to recognize it and resent both the emotion and the source. Second, and more important, she and I sorely need to redefine our somewhat intricate relationship. Two years earlier, when I joined Hilary Ultd. as her secretary, she was definitely boss; I was chattel. But then she learned I have a New York detective's license, and this appealed to her as a frustrated sleuth, so she put me on a more equal footing with the clients. I've suggested we might become partners in a snoop agency like her father's, but she hasn't

8

warmed to the notion yet. Meanwhile, to further strain a taut situation, we have become equal romantic partners and though she hasn't mentioned it, I think Hilary both likes and resents it. She has a profound conviction that all men are out to dominate her, and the fact that I haven't tried probably only suggests to her overly subtle mind that my laissez-faire policy is actually the subtlest of all ploys for gaining psychological ascendancy.

At any rate, at that particular moment, Hilary was in a good humor, thanks to Jack McCabe's risible document. She pointed to article nine (the suggested sequence of toasts) and asked me who Fin was.

"Jimmy Finlayson. He usually played the heavy in Laurel and Hardy pictures. You must have seen him—bald, squint eye, a bushy mustache. He and Charley Hall and Mae Busch were perennial supporting players in their films."

"And Babe? I take it that's Ollie?"

I nodded. "The story is in McCabe's official bio, *Mr. Laurel and Mr. Hardy*. When Hardy was a young movie actor, he used to go to this barber who evidently 'liked boys' and who always used to say 'nice-a baby' whenever he patted powder into Hardy's cheeks. People started to kid him about it and call him 'baby' and eventually the nickname became affectionate and abbreviated—'Babe'—and it stuck."

"You *are* a repository of information," Hilary said, amused and interested. She flicked off the power button of the Adler and gave the machine a rest while she recalled for my benefit the few Laurel and Hardy movies she'd seen, most of them on television.

"It's not fair to evaluate them by what you viewed on the tube," I remarked. "Local stations butcher them, or, even if they run the pictures intact, there are so many commercials stuck in that the timing Stan worked on so hard is totally ruined."

"Stan? You mean Laurel directed the films?"

"Practically. He was the idea man. He invented the gags and at the end of the day, when Babe headed for the golf course, Stan would stay and work with the editor to assure the proper timing of each bit. The main reason the last few pictures the team made were substandard was because M-G-M and 20th

Century-Fox forbid Stan to exercise artistic control over the product."

"I would like to know," Hilary said abruptly, "why you never mentioned the Sons of the Desert to me before. It sounds like a lot of fun. I might like to join."

It was a toucny subject. I steered around it by inviting her to go to the annual banquet in June with me. She accepted with pleasure. Deciding that the time was at last ripe, I asked if she'd mind my taking off a few days to go to Philadelphia.

"Why on earth would you want to do *that*?" Her reaction was that of a typically insular Manhattanite: life anywhere but New York was a hardship. In Philadelphia, it would be positively unthinkable.

I explained that I was a newly elected delegate-at-large for the Sons of the Desert in New York. At the most recent executive committee meeting, I said, the president of the tent, O. J. Wheete, read a letter from the Two Tars tent in Philly proposing a joint regional convention sometime in the fall. "The Two Tars annual banquet is coming up next week," I further explained, "so we figured somebody from our board should go to it and talk about their ideas for such an event."

"But why you? Why not one of the chief officers? Or is a delegate-at-large an important Sons position by some kind of inverted comic logic?"

I shook my head. "That's too subtle for the Sons. Sounds more like Gilbert." As I flipped through the by-law booklet, I told Hilary that I didn't even get a vote at committee meetings. "My main function is to take notes in case other members want to know what the executives are trying to put over on them."

I located the article entitled "Spying customs of the delegates-at-large" and read a few choice passages for Hilary's benefit: "Delegates-at-large . . . will . . . be free to demand large money votes be brought before the general membership. The committee will be free, however, to take exception to such demands by politely escorting the dissenting delegate to the East River.

"Once a year, at the last spring meeting, the delegates-at-large will be elected from the general membership. Nominations will be taken from the floor, where most of the Sons end

10

up, anyway. Election will be determined by voting customs outlined below, or by bribe, whichever comes first. Because success is a rare commodity in the SOTD, delegates-at-large may succeed themselves once.

"Delegates-at-large shall be the chief communications link between members and the committee. Consequently, delegates shall make themselves available to general members for pertinent discussions, provided such demands on time do not extend to The Lambs' rest rooms. However, should a delegate be obliging enough to discuss SOTD business even in the latter contingency, he will be entitled to call himself the Privy Counsellor."

The last clause cracked her up. "All right," Hilary laughed, "you can go, Gene. (Or should I call you John?)" Then she knit her brow. "But you still didn't answer. Why did they pick you instead of the president or another chief officer?"

"Maybe because I'm an ex-Philadelphian. Or maybe because the rest of them wouldn't be caught dead in the City of Brotherly Love."

She shrugged. "The natives would hardly know the difference."

The flippancy annoyed me, but I didn't comment. The more arguments I could avoid with Hilary in the next few weeks, the better.

I knew I was going to need all the goodwill I could get when Hilary found out that the New York parent tent of Sons of the Desert positively refuses to accept women as members.

So:

FADE IN

Long Shot. Interior. Evening.

The main dining room of the Penn Country Club was ostentatious in its lack of ostentation. Sconced wall lights and wine-red textured wallpaper were warm and the overstuffed chairs comfortable.

The meal was at an end, and whatever coffee remained was cold in the cups. The lights were off and some one hundred members of the Two Tars tent watched Laurel and Hardy portray bumbling sailors in the film from which the chapter derives its name.

Guests of honor sat opposite the screen at the head table, which was perpendicular to two long ones; together, the three festive boards comprised a C-shaped mesa of white linen. I was seated with the other guests, feeling uncomfortable in the company of performers like Hurd Hatfield, Mae Questel, and even Wayne Poe. But as emissary from the parent tent, it was my duty to fill a chair and try to look somewhat important.

I was supposed to meet with Jerry Freundlich, the president of the tent, but since he was banquet program co-chairman, he was busy readying the show to be given live after the films, so there was nothing for me to do but relax and enjoy the entertainment.

On the screen, Stan and Ollie engaged in a ridiculous battle with Charley Hall and a gum-ball machine. A few minutes later, they and their dates (Thelma Hill and Ruby Blaine) kicked off one of the most famous sequences in cinematic comedy, the incredibly protracted reciprocal destruction of innumerable stalled automobiles.

The film ended and a specially edited reel followed: it consisted of clips from things our celebrity guests had done. First there was a piece of *The Picture of Dorian Gray*, then a snippet from the NET-TV film *Between Time and Timbuktu*; despite the many years between the two flicks, Hurd Hatfield looked pretty much the same, and someone called out that Hatfield must *really* have a picture in his attic. Next we saw a mercifully brief part of the short-lived *Wayne Poe Show*, a series that had been canceled after six weeks. (The premise: Poe, an effeminate young man, inherited his father's construction firm and had to boss a rowdy crew of *macho* hard-hat laborers.) The film collation closed with a Mae Questel anthology: Betty Boop, a rare "live" appearance with Rudy Vallee; two Popeye scenes, the first with her usual Olive Oyl voice-over, the second, an oddity in which (for matters of studio expedience) she actually read the sailor's lines; the reel ended with "Aunt Bluebell" ringingly urging everyone to "Weigh it for yourself, honey!"

Everyone applauded. The lights came up long enough for the projectionist to change reels and show another Laurel and Hardy short, *The Live Ghost*. When the film ended, there was a burst of music. A three-piece combo which took its place during the blackout played a fanfare. Wayne Poe stepped onto a platform at the far end of the room and introduced himself as master of ceremonies.

Sporadic applause.

He said a few introductory things with a pasted-on grin splitting his mouth so wide I was surprised the corners of his lips didn't crack. He was about thirty-five, not too tall, with thinning auburn hair and black hornrims that made him slightly resemble Jack Benny. Poe's mannerisms were reminiscent of the late lamented comic, but his timing and delivery weren't. He desperately launched one gag right after the last one, never waiting out the laugh properly—when there was one.

He began with approximately one dozen Polish jokes, followed by two Italian gags, one black story, and a pair each of Irish and Jewish anecdotes. By that time, he had offended nearly everyone in the place. Next, he bored us with seven minutes of the same impressions every comedian does— Cagney, Bogey, Lugosi, Cooper, Cary Grant—Xerox copies of

13

carbons, twice removed from reality. Many people were shifting restlessly in their seats by the time Poe launched into a horrendously dragged-out "true" tale of a cocktail waitress he claimed he knew. These were the details, much condensed:

Joan Grablick, the waitress, supplemented her tips by giving shaves and haircuts to her men friends. One day, the owner of the nightclub where she worked heard about his employee's tonsorial skills, so he hired her to give him bi-weekly trims and shaves each morning—all of which greatly augmented her income.

But one fateful day when she was off from work, she stopped into a bowling alley to play a few frames. There she ran into her employer, who was accompanied by a client he was trying to impress. The three of them bowled together and she bettered her boss's score by nearly seventy points. He was so humiliated and angry that he never let her shave him again.

"Which only goes to show," Poe proclaimed at long last, "that a bowling Joan lathers no boss."

Up to then, Poe still had a few people on his side, but the shaggy-dog build-up and the pun finished them off. The audience broke into a chorus of catcalls, hoots, and hisses. Poe responded, predictably enough, with a barrage of insulting one-liners. He might have continued, but when he saw a few people rise, don their coats, and walk out, he decided it was time to give the band the nod for the fanfare that ended his turn.

There was very little applause.

At that moment, I would've wagered there was nothing further Wayne Poe could do to alienate the Two Tars tent. But I would have lost the bet.

He introduced the next act, a gangly, nervous youngster named Bryan Harper—a toothy kid with protruding ears and a ghastly smile that suggested butterflies-in-the-stomach. His black tux looked like it had been supplied by an uncle in the business on Second Avenue. Harper grabbed the mike as if he were afraid it'd slip through his fingers and shatter. He squeaked out the opening lyrics of "They Call the Wind Maria." The choice revealed a colossal case of adolescent wish fulfillment. Not only did he lack the beefiness to color the

14

vowels richly enough, but on the climactic high F, his voice cracked badly.

I felt sorry for the kid. He was rattled, and the audience was not in a good mood. Sparse clapping. He next crooned a simple folk ballad that was more in his range and he did it passingly well. The applause was a little healthier, and he started to relax; the jack-o'-lantern grin melted into a semblance of genuine pleasure, and I thought Harper might make it off with some degree of honor . . .

But when the time came for his upbeat "ride-out" number, he smiled painfully and said he hadn't had a chance to rehearse his last song with the band, but had been advised to go ahead and sing it, anyway, *a cappella*. And with that, he plunged into a truncated version of the excruciatingly difficult Soliloquy from *Carousel*!

I winced. My God! Who was loony enough to put such a dumb idea into Harper's head? To begin with, he couldn't project the virility, and closing any act without the trio would be anticlimactic at best. But for an unsure tyro to attempt a dramatic *tour de force* like Soliloquy that needs the technique of a Rounseville or Tauber to bring off, the choice was artistic suicide.

He didn't even come close. Harper found it hard to keep a steady tempo, and midway through, wandered into the wrong key and way out of his comfortable register. His voice grew shrill, as much from embarrassment as strain. He stopped finally and I thought he was going to apologize and slink away with hung head, but instead he turned to the pianist and asked for a D. The show-must-go-on-I-forget-just-why syndrome.

Somehow, Harper muddled through to the end, but by the time he got there, his eyes were moist with welling tears. He hurried offstage, head down, taking quick strides to get away as fast as possible. He didn't dignify the fiasco by returning to acknowledge the compassionate applause.

And then, just then, before the clapping died away, Wayne Poe bounced back onstage. He nodded to the band—and I suddenly had an awful premonition of what he was about to do.

I was right: the combo hit a B-chord and stayed with Poe as he resang the last fifteen or twenty bars of the same Soliloquy. He wasn't much of a singer, but *he* was accompanied, and anything had to sound better than the musical mayhem committed by Harper.

It was the rottenest trick I'd ever seen pulled. Another audience might have been taken in by it, but the Two Tars group is too savvy. When Poe finished, there wasn't a single sound, not even that of one hand clapping.

And then the stony silence was shattered by a new voice, a loud, raucous one. It came from the shadows behind the platform.

"HEY, BOY! GET YOUR ASS OFFSTAGE! THE OLD MAN'S TAKING OVER!!!"

Poe swiveled, gawking at the spectacle emerging into the spotlight's spill. It was Frank Butler, a short man with a big potbelly, massive forehead and jaw, and downturned lips from which stuck out an evil-looking, twisted stogie. Wisps of graying hair were carefully plastered over his balding skull. As he clumped onto the platform, I noticed he was carrying a large, floppy object that looked like a miniature corpse dangling its grotesque limbs.

It was a ventriloquist's figure, a dummy fashioned to resemble W. C. Fields.

When the Two Tars saw it, a great collective groan rose from many throats. Butler, who showed no sign of having heard, tromped to the microphone, deliberately planted his feet squarely behind it and opened his mouth to speak. I figured he was going to apologize for Poe.

Instead, he belched.

"Sorry," he grumbled, "good eats." He regarded Poe frostily. "Lookit, boy, *I* gotta save this show! You shoved it right where I stick Sani-Flush!"

Poe stared in blank amazement. Who *was* this idiotic amateur?! The comedian's mouth opened in protest, but whatever he was going to say was drowned in Butler's peremptory bellow.

"Get me that chair, boy! I'll show you how to entertain!"

As he said it, the leader of the combo leaned over and whispered to the other instrumentalists. Maybe he was ashamed of what he'd done to Harper; at any rate, Poe's next retort went

16

unheard because the band suddenly blared out the first strain of "The Entertainer" triple fortissimo.

Poe jumped off the platform, grabbed the indicated chair, and hauled it up as he mounted the stage again. He held it for Butler, but just as the ventriloquist's ample butt neared the seat, Poe yanked it away. Butler hit the floor with a wham.

There was scattered laughter, but the most audible sound was the colorful stream of remarks uttered by Frank Butler.

He and Poe wrangled as Butler scrambled to his feet. Then, shoving the comic to one side, Butler motioned for the band to fade out. He started his routine.

Poe did not leave the platform, as he should have—whatever the group thought of Butler, it had had enough of Poe. But he remained there, glowering. His presence clearly boded Butler no good.

But Butler ignored him, now that he was embarked on his vent act. As a performer, he was creatively putrid, and he sounded about as much like W. C. Fields as I resemble Hilary's fat father.

Dummy: You ever hear the expression, "A little knowledge is a dangerous thing?"
Butler: Yep.
Dummy: Well, relax, you're practically invulnerable!
Or:
Dummy: I know a man who bought a no-nose goat.
Butler: If the goat doesn't have a nose, how does he smell?
Dummy: TERRIBLE!
Yuk, yuk, yuk.

Not only did the material stink, but Butler didn't come anywhere near imitating Fields's incomparable drawl/whine. Furthermore, he didn't know how to coordinate the dummy's jaw movements with the words. On the other hand, Butler's lips flapped so much that his cigar waggled up and down like a baton.

He was so unashamedly inept that I found him perversely funny. However, the rest of the group must have been treated to far too liberal a share of Franklin Butler's questionable talents on past occasions. There was grumbling, fidgeting, and a lot of extraneous talking.

17

When Butler finally stashed the dummy under the chair, he swung into the "joke" portion of his act. His mode of presentation consisted of rooting around in his pockets for dingy 3x5 file cards on which he had written various punch lines as memory aids. After the umpteenth story, he put away the cards and announced he was about to close his act—

(Loud cheers)

—"with some *real* singing!"

An universal groan.

Imagine the noise of an alleycat indulging unwillingly in a *ménage à trois* in the middle of a marble factory and you will have evoked a faint notion of the unique caliber and timbre of Franklin Butler's lusty rendition of "Last Night I Stayed Up Late," which he shouted to the tune of "Funiculi, Funicula."

I noticed Wayne Poe finally quitting the platform, a wild look in his eye. He dashed out of the room.

Without pause, Butler segued into a medley of bawdy parodies of all-time-favorite song hits. The most innocuous was:

> Oh, give me a home where the beer bottles foam
> And the blondes and the redheads all play;
> Where seldom is heard a discouraging word
> 'Cause my wife is out hustling all day.

I figured Poe couldn't stand the noise. Neither could anyone else. Some people started getting on their coats. Hardier (drunker) souls took up a chorus of jeering to drown him out, but he just got louder.

And then Wayne Poe came back. Heads turned as one person after the other nudged his neighbor and pointed to the comic. Poe had something behind his back and was sidling up to the platform without showing what he was holding.

Just as Frank Butler vigorously began the opening verse of "The Bastard King of England," Poe bounded onto the platform and whipped out two objects he had been concealing. The first, a pair of scissors, he used to sever the singer's microphone cord.

It didn't help much. Butler was too loud. However, Poe's

next action was much more ameliorative. Butler found it decidedly difficult to continue the song while a stream of seltzer water was being directed into his big mouth. He replaced the rowdy lyric with a generous mixture of sputtering and swearing.

Poe's stratagem had an electric effect upon the remaining members of the company. The audience rose in one corporate body and applauded, stomped, yelled "bravo," and in general produced an enormous quantity of noise.

Poe smiled his Cheshire-cat grin and bowed. Which was a mistake. It presented an irresistible target to the outraged performer behind him. Poe sprawled on his face on the floor in front of the platform.

I told the story to a couple of the Sons in New York, and they agreed it was the best way to get Wayne Poe offstage.

Camac Street is not the worst street in Philly, but it would place amongst the ten finalists. What it lacks in picturesqueness, it more than makes up for in narrowness. Maybe two pygmies *can* walk abreast in the middle of it, but it would help if they were both narrow-shouldered.

The most famous commercial establishment on the street is the Camac Baths, a combination Russian-Turkish steambath known to local clientele as the *shvitz*, or, in rough translation, "the place where one sweats." Less than two blocks away, on the same side of the street, there is a dilapidated town house with a weather-worn sign jutting over the entranceway to identify the sole occupant:

DJINN INVESTIGATIONS INC.
B. F. Butler, proprietor.

I had planned to talk about the regional convention with Jerry Freundlich, president of the Two Tars tent. But after the Butler-Poe battle, he was so busy assuaging feelings, apologizing to members and guests, and in general doing what he could to avoid lawsuits, that he asked me to go along with Butler and get the pertinent details from him.

It was in his decrepit Packard that Butler mentioned his occupation. I might have gagged, but at the moment I was too busy white-knuckling the dashboard and the edge of my seat, whatever I could wrap my hands around.

Butler drove like a hotfooted demon. He confided he once drove race cars, and his biggest ambition was to raise enough scratch to compete at Le Mans. Meanwhile, until he realized his dream, he pushed the poor heap to the limit of endurance, hairpinning corners, weaving intricate curlicues around the center line of the road, braking unmercifully and capriciously. The wind whipping into the car ruffled up the sparse graying hair from his head, revealing the bald pate that Butler took pains to minimize.

"Just wait'll I fix that crap Poe!" he snarled, tromping on the brakes so hard I almost sailed through the windshield.

"Take it easy! You almost gave me a concussion!"

"Sorry, my nerves're jumpy, boy. Open the glove compartment and grab me a tranquilizer."

The "tranquilizer" turned out to be a pint of Colt 45, one of five cans of it stored where he told me to look. The empty sixth can on the floorboard rolled back and forth under my feet. The glove compartment was stuffed with road maps, greasy rags, and debris which turned out to be pieces of walnut shells.

I tried to dissuade Butler from drinking while driving, but he snatched the can from my grip and scowled.

"Hell, boy, this ain't drinkin'! When we get over to my place, I'll show you drinkin'!" He guzzled the malt beverage.

His place turned out to be the dingy walk-up on Camac Street. It took us a good hour to reach it from the country club, even with his supersonic-speed driving. (I had to admit to myself he took it easier once he'd gotten his mitts on the brew, but I was damned if I'd give verbal sanction to the harrowing habit.)

The car scraped to a stop along the curb and Butler lumbered out. I followed him as he wobbled down the street in a pattern reminiscent of the way he drove the Packard. Every other step or so, he mumbled something derogatory about Wayne Poe beneath his breath.

(Later I learned the only reason Poe had been asked to appear at the Two Tars dinner was because he'd been recommended to Butler by O. J. Wheete, president of the SOTD parent tent. It figured; O. J. would probably find something nice to say about Jesse James while handing the outlaw his wallet.)

Butler led me up a narrow stairway past empty flats that probably once were places of business. At the top, on the wall, I saw a sign, DJINN INVESTIGATIONS INC., with an arrow pointing to the sole door on that level. There was a bell-push in the portal, but it hung loose, gutted.

Unlocking the door, he motioned me through a cramped green room which he called his office. He parted a dusty bead curtain, flicked on the lights, unstrapped his belt and tossed it in a corner, then invited me into a chilly chamber with patches of plaster peeping out of holes in the wallpaper. It was furnished only by a cot, a table and a few chairs, a hassock, a battered old bureau, and an open safe stuffed with walnuts. There was a great quantity of cobweb and grime and the room stank of cigars.

"You live here?" I asked, incredulous.

Butler shrugged, scratching his ample belly. "Family pressures. I keep this place handy when it gets too hot at home. How 'bout some gin?"

I declined. He shook his head, unable to understand my lack of interest in juniper juice. He extracted a pint from the safe, plunked it on the table, and repeated the question, or so I erroneously thought. I mentioned I'd already had enough to drink, but he shook his head and pulled some cards from his pocket—not the 3x5s with punch lines, but a greasy, dog-eared regulation poker pack.

"Wanna *play* gin?" he elucidated.

I said yes. This was a mistake. In the next two hours, Butler consumed a pint of gin, half a dozen cigars, an innumerable amount of walnuts, and approximately one-fifth of my week's salary.

I didn't actually see him pull anything funny, but gin is a game eminently suited to cardsharping. You don't have to deal with a mechanic's grip to control the flow of fortune. The ratio of luck to skill is about equal, so anything, no matter how slight, which tips the scale in favor of one player provides him an enormous advantage. I'm sure Butler wasn't dealing out of the middle, but it was his deck and he might have been able to recognize certain cards from the peculiar striations and bends that age had marked them with. Of course, the condition of the cards could have worked to my advantage, too, after a few hands—except for the insane gin rummy convention that the winner, rather than the loser, deals the next hand.

Having agreed to play, I deserved what I got. I was only angry at myself for not declining the game as soon as I got a glimpse of Butler's cards. But my brain doesn't function at its best late at night.

Butler further befuddled me with a smokescreen, both literal and figurative. His cigars made my eyes smart, and the continual cracking of walnuts began to separate the lobes of my brain into two neat hemispheres. All the while, he kibitzed about the proposed plans for the New York Philly joint SOTD convention in the fall. Since this conversation was the chief reason I'd come to Pennsylvania, I had to pay attention, even though it further interfered with my already impaired card sense.

"We'll throw the whole blast at Valley Forge, if that's okay with you. There's a good place there, cheap, plenty room." He paused to swig gin. "You'll hafta charter a bus to bring down your members. Whaddaya say?"

C-r-r-rack.

"I'll bring it up at the executive committee meeting next week," I replied, throwing away a deuce.

"Gimme!" He swooped down on it; Butler had a habit of picking up my discards. "How about if I drive up to New York next week and sit in on that session, get things done faster, how's that sound?"

C-r-r-rack.

"Sounds fine to me."

"Swell, boy, I'll be there. Gin."

I paid off while he munched walnuts.

By the time we called it quits, it was nearly light out. I hastily declined his offer to drive me to my hotel. I needed the fresh air, and if there were any muggers still awake, I figured I had a better chance of survival with them than with Butler's driving.

I didn't want to insult him, but I felt I needed to know the truth. As I pulled on my topcoat, I asked him point-blank if he'd been cheating. "I won't get mad if the answer's yes, I just want to know why I didn't spot it if you were. You didn't false-shuffle or misdeal. The only thing I can figure is you recognize some of the cards by their backs."

He chortled in his joy. "So the Old Man's too sharp for you,

23

hey, boy? Tell you what . . . you bring your own deck next week, and I'll play you again. Fair enough?''

I nodded.

Butler flopped down on the cot and started pulling off his shoes and socks. "Like some friendly advice, boy?''

"What is it?''

"Like Mark Twain says, 'I was a stranger and they took me in . . .' " He gave me a broad wink and grinned.

The attribution was wrong, but I got the point of the quote.

The executive committee, hereinafter known as "the committee" or as "those loud bastards at the corner table," shall consist of the officers, past presidents, heads of standing committees and del-egates-at-large. The latter will only be seated if they are not too fat to squeeze in and if they can refrain from constant catcalls. General members may attend individual committee meetings if they are invited by the president, or if they plan to buy booze all around.
—from *The Sons of the Desert Guidelines to Decorous Behaviour (by-laws)*

According to the postcard O. J. mailed me, the meeting would begin at 7:30 P.M. Wednesday. That evening, I turned off Broadway and took my time strolling east on 44th. It was ten minutes before eight, but I wasn't worried about being late.

Halfway down the block, I entered the sedate building that housed The Lambs and nodded to the doorkeeper. It was a balmy evening in May, so I hung my coat in the foyer before proceeding into the still-bustling dining room.

It was a warm, festive place, festooned with brass plaques, pewter drinking cups, and oil paintings of former Shepherds of the club, as well as pictures, letters, and similar memorabilia of members, past and present. The dark wood paneling resembled the interior of an Austrian tavern. I never tired of wandering through the restaurant and adjacent bar/game room, reading framed theatrical programs, picking out the faces of character actors, comedians, singers, and dancers of my youth in the fading photographs. At the rear of the bar and beyond it was an immense curved seat capable of holding quite a few people. A great number of caricatures of various Lambs celebrities were suspended above it; the artists were all popular cartoonists of days gone by.

It was here that the Sons executive committee convened. "RACK 'EM!"

Our own popular cartoonist, Al Kilgore, the satanically bearded co-founder and Grand Sheik of the Sons of the Desert, brandished his pool cue like a weapon and repeated his stentorian suggestion. His powerful voice overrode somebody's single-fingered piano rendition of Laurel and Hardy's whimsical motto theme, "The Cuckoo Song," and also drowned out Phil Faxon's whiskey-tenor caroling of "Blue Ridge Mountains of Virginia." The mirror behind the bar trembled with the force of Kilgore's outburst.

The other delegate-at-large, Toby Sanders, a professional clown, took off the jacket of his mocha leisure suit, draped it over a chair, and started assembling the billiard balls in the triangle. Kilgore positioned himself at the other end of the table for the break. They made an interesting contrast: Kilgore, tall, robust, forceful; Toby, diminutive and diffident.

Across the room, our ex-president, Tye Morrow, head of an important Manhattan tour-guide agency, entered, removed a gold cigarette case from his pocket and took a weed and fitted it into an elegant holder. He nodded hello to Phil Faxon, one of our more impecunious members, and automatically bought him a drink.

At a small round bar table next to where Phil was sitting, O. J. quietly but determinedly disagreed with our treasurer, Natie, over an expenditure incurred by the vice-president, Hal Fawkes. Our ex-treasurer, Barry Richmond, hung over the back of the chair of his successor and kibitzed the argument.

Natie Barrows, a short and stocky actor, has wiry hair and too many teeth which are always displayed in a nervous grin. He's one of those people who wants to be liked even if he disagrees to the point of calling you names. That night, he had on a tweed jacket (a begrudging concession to Lambs' dress code), but beneath it was his standard mufti, an orange T-shirt on which was emblazoned a picture, I swear, of Mary Tyler Moore, Natie's *belle dame sans merci*.

O. J. was waiting for Hal Fawkes and Dutchy Hovis to arrive before getting under way. Hal, our VP, was actually in the lobby, but he was making his usual series of last-minute phone calls. Dutchy, when he came at all, was invariably late.

It was five after eight, thirty-five minutes later than announced, and the meeting had not yet begun. Right on time for the executive committee.

The smoky atmosphere was already starting to tenderize my head for the inevitable dull headache I would walk out with. I carried my Bushmills/rocks and Beck's chaser to the right end seat of the circular table. It was the best place for me, because I wouldn't bump anyone with my writing arm when I took minutes. (It wasn't my job, but the recording secretary—or, to use his official title, The Moving Finger—was a phantom. He never showed. O. J. should have replaced him, but I think I mentioned our chief officer is too benign to kick people in the pants, so we dragged the dead weight of the delinquent's name along on our letterhead, and I filled in temporarily. O. J. said he was going to nominate me for the post the next time we had an election.) I was just about to sit and take out my notebook when a bellow from the part of the room where the pool tables stood drew my attention.

"What the holy hell're you *doing*?" Al Kilgore demanded, momentarily stopping all activity in the bar. Heads turned. Necks craned.

I walked over to see what was happening. Al and his pool partner, Toby, had been playing, but now a pair of newcomers had joined to make it a team competition. One of the two was our tardy member, Dutchy Hovis, a big, floppy, secretive ex-pugilist with high forehead, nose squashed from too many prizefights, and loose, smiling lips. Dutchy made a pretense of being jolly-fellow-slap-on-the-back, but it was a technique for holding the rest of us off at arm's-length from the inner man, whoever that was.

The other new pool player was short, fat, semibald. At that moment, he sprawled across the pool table with his cue-stick in hand. When he saw me, he popped up for a second and waved jauntily.

"Hey, boy, how's your ass?" he asked in a voice as rock-shattering as Kilgore's.

Frank Butler was evidently very much inebriated.

I asked Toby what Kilgore was sore about.

27

"These two just came in and challenged us to a partnership game of 8-Ball."

"So?"

"So," Kilgore snapped, "I drew this cat as a partner." He jerked his finger at Butler. "I mean, what the hell is *this*?"

The *this* to which he referred was the fact that Butler was aiming his shot directly at the 8-ball. Since both sides still had several other numbers to sink, it was the wrong target; if it dropped into a pocket prematurely, the game would be immediately forfeit for the Butler/Kilgore side.

"Butler," I murmured, "just what the hell *are* you trying to do?"

"Oh, boy, don't you see the strategy?" Butler asked, aggrieved. "Look at that now!" He pointed to a 4-ball far on the other side of the black 8. "That's their next target. Now there's no way I can drop our side's ball this shot, so all I'm gonna do is maybe nudge the 8-ball a little closer to the side pocket and make their turn that much tougher." He spread his hands wide and grinned at the ingenious logic, the pure poetry of his decision.

"I don't *believe* this bugger!" Kilgore groaned. "I mean, what *is* this?"

I suggested to Butler that if he misjudged, he'd put the 8-ball in the pocket and lose the game for him and his partner.

"Haw!" he snorted, hunching over the table for his shot. "You gotta trust the Old Man!" He drew back the tip of the cue-stick and almost flopped onto the cloth. I caught him and planted his feet on the wooden flooring so he wouldn't topple. Butler brushed me away and warmed up again.

"Don't do it!" Kilgore pleaded. Toby laughed at his opponent's plight.

Butler took the shot. The stick hit the white ball; it shot forward, clipping the 8-ball as it went. The black ball wobbled laterally, ambling in the direction of the side pocket. It reached the lip of the hole, teetered, righted itself—

"*See?*" the old curmudgeon crowed. "*You gotta know how to apply English!*"

—and plopped into the pocket.

28

Kilgore knocked the flat of his palm against his forehead while Dutchy Hovis cackled with delight.

"I don't *believe* that cat!" Kilgore repeated, over and over again.

Toby, who was twice as shy as O. J., murmured under his breath that Butler's play was the stupidest pool decision he'd ever seen in his life.

"That's because he's sloshed," Dutchy Hovis said, leaning over Toby's shoulder. "Normally, the Old Man's pretty sharp."

"Try telling that to Al," I said.

Curiously, Butler didn't seem particularly abashed about the outcome of his pool tactics. He even agreed to pay the whole bet himself.

"You better," Al grumbled. "You expect me to pay for that piece of stuff?" Our Grand Sheik was understandably perturbed, and his language was a bit more blunt than I'm bothering to report.

The forfeit was to buy the others a round at the bar. Al asked for a beer, but Dutchy, opportunist that he was, ordered a Glenfiddich Scotch, the most expensive sold at The Lambs. I helped Butler over to the bar since he was still shaky on his legs. Toby started racking the balls for a new game, and Kilgore protested that he wasn't having Butler as a partner again.

Just then, O. J. stood up and cleared his throat. "All right, gentlemen, everyone's here. Meeting time."

"Oh, Christ, *already*?" Hal Fawkes blurted out. "I gotta make a phone call."

"You've made at least thirty," Natie argued. "C'mon, we'll *never* get finished!"

Hal shook his grizzled head. "Can't wait. Be right back." He headed for the phones again, nearly tripping en route.

The rest of us started to take our places at the big semicircular seat, setting drinks on the enormous round tabletop. Tye Morrow brought over a huge platter of crackers and cheese spread and placed it in the center so everyone could help himself. Kilgore put his cue-stick away a little reluctantly. Barry Richmond asked me if I minded his sitting next to me, and I swiveled my legs out long enough for His Excellency to squeeze in. (The

29

title went with his self-bestowed position of President of Montmartre. Barry is tall, gangly, and wears glasses with a built-in snigger; he looks like an older Tony Perkins from *Psycho*, and Kilgore frequently calls him "Norman" after the disturbed motel keeper in that film.)

Eight of us occupied the great arc of the large seat. To my left, next to Barry, sat Phil Faxon, a character actor who was one of the damnedest vocal mimics I'd ever heard. Thin, sandy-haired, with weak eyes (and no spectacles), Faxon could imitate accurately anyone from Herbert Hoover to Charles Laughton, but only with his voice, not his body. If radio were only still an important dramatic medium, he'd be rich, but as it was, he earned what income he did from an occasional voice-over for a TV commercial, or a narration for an army training movie.

O. J. sat to his left, his mild blue eyes scanning the company, fingers tapping the neatly inscribed memorandum book he used for running meetings. Too well-mannered to hurry the start of proceedings, he displayed his impatience to those who knew him well enough by the involuntary tapping. But his face gave away nothing.

Next to O. J. was Natie Barrows, our treasurer. Though he still had an automatic grin on his face, Natie was busily and anxiously wiping off a wayward gob of cheese from Mary Tyler Moore's nose on his sweatshirt. To Natie's left, Al Kilgore watched the loving ministration with undisguised astonishment. Beside Al sat Toby Sanders, dwarfed by his neighbor, and on the far end opposite me, Frank Butler perched, bald spot neatly concealed by his carefully combed hair fringe. He puffed away at one of his odd-looking, peculiarly aromatic stogies.

There was no room left for Dutchy or Tye, so they pushed wooden curved-back chairs to the end of the table, including one for Hal, if he ever decided to return.

At that particular moment, waiting for O. J. to begin the meeting, few of us had Wayne Poe in mind, I'm sure. Even with hindsight, it probably never has occurred to most of the SOTD executive committee that the murder of Wayne Poe was first conceived and plotted during that very meeting.

30

If there is ever a normal committee meeting, the order of business will be as follows: 1. The president will call the meeting to order (beer, Scotch, etc.). 2. The treasurer will apologize. 3. Heads of standing committees will proffer excuses for their inefficiency. 4. Old business will be dragged out, dusted off and lovingly tabled for a future meeting. 5. New business must be tabled as soon as possible, in order that it may be brought up at a future meeting as old business. 6. The president shall then inform members of the committee that while they were at the bar and/or pool tables, the meeting ended. 7. At the discretion of the president—a concept which will be theoretically, though laughingly granted—the above order of business may be hopelessly screwed up.
    —from *The Sons of the Desert Guidelines to Decorous Behaviour (by-laws)*

O. J. began with new business, backtracked into old, forgot to ask for committee and treasurer reports entirely, and didn't let me read the minutes or talk about the Two Tars convention plans.

"Gentlemen," he said, "Frank Butler came all the way from Philadelphia to tell us about the joint meeting."

Everyone listened respectfully, with the possible exception of Al Kilgore.

"We gotta forget about a September bash," Butler stated. "No convention facilities available. But we can grab the Village Inn in Valley Forge right after July 4th." He waved down the gabble of protest. "Yeah, yeah, I know! But our board says we can slap the whole shindig together, program, eats, and booze, and all you birds gotta do is find a way to come. Charter a bus."

Natie interrupted. "That's hardly four weeks after our own

31

banquet, we can't rent a bus, the treasury'll be flat busted!'' He always fought losing battles on overextension of club funds. It helped account for the upset stomachs and the perennial tense smile Natie had, caused by his pathetic desire to be liked, and his self-annoyance at the trait. In our committee debates, he was usually ignored unless he threw a temper tantrum.

The great transportation debate continued. Dutchy suggested five dollars be added on to the cost of every banquet ticket to help pay for the bus.

Phil grumbled, ''I can't afford it as it is *now*.''

O. J. mentioned that the tickets were already printed.

''So run off a new batch,'' Dutchy said. He was always willing to volunteer more work for other people.

At that point, there was much arguing and Dutchy's proposal was worried to shreds. Natie tried to get a word in, but O. J. didn't notice the treasurer's politely upraised hand with everyone else arguing at once. Natie's face grew redder and redder. At last, he slammed the big Sons checkbook on the table and screamed for the others to shut up.

The Lambs bartender requested that Natie lower *his* voice.

''We can't afford new tickets,'' Natie said, half mumbling, his cheeks flushed with anger and embarrassment.

Dutchy sneered. ''Whatcha doin' with the treasury, buying a refrigerator to keep MTM in?''

''Damn it,'' said Natie, ''I just pay the bills. Talk to O. J. or Hal about running them up!''

O. J. quickly and deftly steered the discussion away from financial matters by observing that he wanted to get home by eleven o'clock to tape the soundtrack of *Broadway Thru a Keyhole* on WOR-TV. The art of channeled digression. It got the buffs onto a ten-minute tangent concerning the brief career of Russ Columbo.

When the original subject was returned to, it was agreed (mostly out of exhaustion) that the Two Tars would proceed with convention plans and the parent tent would discuss transportation another day. Natie looked very dubious.

I said I'd inform Butler of the decision when he woke. His head was flat on the table; he snored. Toby moved his tie out of the cheese spread.

"All right, gentlemen," said O. J., "the main topic tonight is the June banquet. The Laurel and Hardy film this year, with your sanction, will be *The Hoose-Gow*. Fin has a good part in it, Charley Hall has a bit, too. As for Mae—listen to this! We're actually going to see what there is left of *The Knifethrower*!"

"WOW!"

Everyone babbled excitedly. Dutchy whistled. "How'd you run it down?" he asked. Nostalgia was the only area he ever opened up on. "I thought it was gone for good."

"Hal found it."

"Where?"

"He's got sources," O. J. replied. "Who knows—"

"—what evil lurks in the hearts of men? The Shadow knows!" Phil Faxon sneered in a sinister timbre.

The entire committee joined him in an imitation of the invisible crime-fighter's memorably aquilinic snigger.

"To continue," O. J. chuckled, "at the banquet we will have on the podium, Bob and Ray once more, Rodney Dangerfield, our own Chuck McCann, and Butterfly McQueen—"

"What she gwine t'do?" Phil laughed. "Sing 'n' dance?"

No one said anything, but several reproving glances were cast in his direction. Phil, nearing sixty, was apparently suffering hardening of the prejudices.

O. J. mentioned a few other "iffy" possibles for the head table, then proudly announced, "I have one more piece of excellent news, gentlemen . . . the most important thing of all! This year, the annual Sons comedy plaque will be given to Billy White and Jack Black!"

"Goddelmighty," Natie said, awestruck, "they must both be ninety!"

O. J. shook his head. "Jack's ninety-two, but Billy's only eighty-seven."

"*Only*?"

We were all impressed. Though I'm younger than most of the board, I remember comedy appearances on early TV of Black and White, "America's oldest, funniest vaudeville stars." They dated back to 1900 or thereabouts. White was British, like Stan, but lost his accent and music-hall style in Second Avenue burlesque, Coney Island carnival, vaudeville, et cetera. He

33

met Jack Black at Minsky's, where Black was a candy butcher. They shaped up a two-act PDQ and soon became a headlining team.

"Both of them," O. J. told us, "now live upstate at the AGVA retirement home. We'll rent a limousine—"

Natie groaned.

"—pick them up, then take 'em back afterwards. Of course, if the weather's rough, they'll have to cancel, but otherwise—"

"Forget the otherwise," said a new voice. "They're *not* coming!"

It was our VP, Hal—at long last back from the phone booths. A chunky man about 5-foot-7, he has a head of grizzled gray hair that looks like a used Brillo pad. I would have suspected a hairpiece except for the dandruff flecks that he scratches from his scalp and, after a quick, furtive inspection, flicks to the floor. He sat down between Dutchy and Tye, barking his shins on the table leg in the process. Reaching for crackers and cheese, he managed to decorate his cuff with an aromatic smear of the latter substance.

"What do you mean, they're not coming?" O. J. echoed, stunned.

"Just what I said," Hal mumbled through a mouthful of Keeblers. I turned away, not willing to study the open spectacle of teeth and masticated Saltines.

Hal has a habit of dropping bombshells casually at committee meetings, then staring abstractedly into space, as if unaware of the weight of the pronouncement he's made. At last, under the impatient prompting of the board, he said he'd talked to the nurse at the AGVA home and learned that Billy White had suffered a mild stroke. He was in fair condition, but it was extremely unlikely that'd he be going anyplace in the next few weeks.

"What about Jack?" O. J. anxiously asked. "Couldn't he accept the plaque for both of them?"

"I dunno," Hal said, swallowing a mouthful of cracker. He complained it was too dry. Tye rose, went to the bar and bought him a drink. Meanwhile, Hal admitted he hadn't considered the possibility of bringing just Jack Black down. "I thought you wanted the two of them."

34

"Well, certainly," O. J. said, "but if it's not possible, Jack can take the place of both. In fact, he's the one we really *need*. You know how sharp he still is? He agreed to do a part in the skit we're getting ready."

"At *his* age?" Natie asked, startled. "Sure it's safe?"

"His doctor said the mental challenge'll be good for Jack, provided he gets plenty of rest before and after."

"Well, so be it," Dutchy Hovis said. "Hal, get the home back on the horn and ask Jack if he'll come by himself."

"He's liable to be asleep by now," someone observed.

"Never!" It was Tye Morrow. He set the drink in front of Hal Fawkes. "Jack is probably still up chasing nurses."

Hal said he'd call Black as soon as he finished his drink. In the meantime, we discussed what to do if Jack Black said no. At the least, that would mean scrapping the ten-minute pantomime playlet which the old man was supposed to participate in. There just wouldn't be enough time to find someone else to replace Black.

Phil Faxon said he could fill in with twenty minutes of radio and film sound-track imitations, but O. J. patted his hand and diplomatically said he didn't want to spoil Phil's evening by asking him to get up and perform again.

"I know what *I* could do!" Barry Richmond grinned, his black-framed glasses glinting in the artificial light.

"We all know what you can do, Norman!" Al Kilgore answered. "Go back to the motel and wash out the shower!"

"No, really," Barry insisted, "there's one thing that bugs me. Nobody ever gets my title right! Every time I set up the lights or build the stage platform for a banquet show, what happens? Somebody puts my name in the program wrong."

He wasn't being all that serious, but O. J. couldn't politely refuse the gambit, so he asked Barry what the trouble was.

"The last program referred to me as 'Lighting Designer, The Hon. Barry A. Richmond.' "

"What's wrong with that, Hon?" Natie cooed in a grotesque parody of flirtatiousness.

"As president of Montmartre, I insist on correct proto-col—"

"Barry," Tye Morrow interrupted, with some severity,

35

"you've been complaining about this for three years now, and still nobody knows what you're talking about."

"And I don't want to know," Kilgore laughed.

"I don't blame you " Barry agreed, "I don't know what I'm talking about myself."

"Hear, hear," Natie chimed in. "All in favor of Barry not explaining what he's talking about, say 'Aye.' "

A nearly unanimous chorus.

"Nay?"

"*Nay.*" Every eye turned in the direction of the murmured sound.

"Toby," Dutchy yelped, "are you outta your bird?"

"Barry's always talking about his correct titles," Toby protested. "I want to hear what they are, finally. All of them."

"*All* of them?" Barry gawked.

Toby nodded.

"Okay," Barry sighed, rooting through his briefcase, "here goes . . ."

At those magic words, nearly everybody got up.

"RACK 'EM!"

"Who wants another refill?"

"I gotta take a leak."

O. J., Barry, Toby, and I stayed, but everyone else moved in all possible directions at once. The bustle of bodies roused Frank Butler, who'd been snoring for some time.

"Hey, boy, what's up? Meeting over?"

"Not yet." I shook my head. "Just a recess."

"Recess, hell!" Barry objected. "This is for the minutes." He consulted a paper withdrawn from his briefcase. "My complete title is—His Excellency Sir Barry Alan Richmond, Knight Bachelor, Night Errant, Order Cross Lorraine, Order of the Brutish Umpire; President of the Serene Republic of Montmartre and her Dependencies; Supreme Commander-in-Chief of the Armed Forces, Defender of the Faith and God's Middle Finger on Earth—"

The last one fetched a whoop from Toby, but Barry went on, obliviously. "Chief Magistrate, Emperor of Montmartre Possessions in India, China and the Ottoman Empire, Co-Prince of the Valleys and Suzerainties of Andorra, Doge of Little Italy,

No-Account of Monte Cristo, High Muckamuck, Thane of Cawdor, Grand Bastard of Flanders, High Priest of the Effluent Society and Most Grand and Exalted Ruler of the Ancient and Worshipful Guild of Gongfemors—''

"What in holy mouthwash is *that*?" Butler growled.

"Latin for *sewer cleaners*. Bey of Prigs, Dey of Reckoning, Chief of State of the Montmartre Community/Commonwealth and Greater North American Co-Prosperity Sphere—''

Toby, who'd kicked the whole thing off in the first place, shook his head, rose, and, squeezing past Butler, hurried in the direction of the men's room.

"But there's more!" Barry called after his retreating back. "Grand Panjandrum and Seneschal of Montmartre, Protector of the Hairy Ainus and three South American tribes—''

"Huh?" It was O. J.

"I don't know their names. One tribe can't speak at all, the second only talks through its noses, and in the third, the men and women speak different languages and understand each other only with a lot of difficulty.''

"Barry," O. J. begged, "that's enough."

"There isn't much more. Great Mogul of Montmartre, High Constable, High Sheriff, Marshall of Eastern Rumelia, Regent of the Duchy of Finkelstein—''

There was a loud noise at the other end of the table. Barry and I looked over at Frank Butler. He had just clomped an ancient, rusty .45 on the table in front of him.

"You nearly done?" he asked calmly.

"Leader-of-Men-Seducer-of-Women-and-General-All-Around-Nice-Guy-*that's-it*!" Barry rattled off the words so fast they ran into each other. Then, from the corner of his mouth, he told me to get the hell up so he could push past and take himself out of Butler's vicinity.

We both rose, leaving Butler alone with O. J. That was a big mistake. If I'd stayed, I might have saved Wayne Poe's life— admittedly a doubtful honor.

When the committee sat back down, O. J. dropped a bombshell. "Gentlemen, Frank Butler here has suggested we get Wayne Poe to appear at our banquet. If Jack Black can't make it, he could fill in beautifully.''

Loud protests. Angry words. I stared at Butler, wondering why he'd proposed his nemesis of the scissors-and-seltzer-bottle. I was sure that Butler, once crossed, wouldn't tend to forget a grudge. I suspected a plot.

Butler held up his hand for silence. "Listen, boys," he said, lighting a cigar, "Poe was the hit of the Two Tars show. Everybody stood up and clapped."

Was Frank Butler drunker than I'd realized?

"Wayne Poe," Natie emphatically stated, "is a first-class son-of-a-bitch! Somebody ought to break his neck!"

Dutchy seconded the sentiment.

Phil Faxon observed that if Wayne Poe dropped dead immediately, it would be too soon.

"He's right," said Natie. "Everybody in favor of Wayne Poe dropping dead, say 'Aye.' "

"AYE!" The voice vote was nearly unanimous.

"You're not supposed to vote," Al Kilgore told Toby.

"For *this*, he should be allowed," Natie said.

O. J. argued about having Poe on the show with us. Now as long as the question didn't actually get put to a vote, I knew O. J. would do as he pleased. He actually liked Poe. Since I could not, as a delegate-at-large, propose the motion to ban the comic, the next-best thing I could do was to relate my version of what really happened in Philadelphia.

But I didn't get a chance. Hal Fawkes reappeared and when O. J. saw him, he seized the opportunity to change the subject.

"Well? Did you get hold of Jack Black?"

Hal nodded. He plopped in his chair, catching the pocket of his jacket on the wooden arm, ripping it. He cursed.

"Come on, Hal!" Natie prompted. "Don't make us pry it out of you!"

"I've got him holding, O. J.," Hal said, ruefully fingering his jacket. "He's not so sure he should come now, so maybe you better talk to him. Last booth over."

O. J. rose and went to the lobby and the telephone. We all held our breaths.

"If Jack doesn't come," Hal said, "we'll hafta scrap the film clip of him and Billy."

"Film clip, hell," said Barry, "we'll have to line up a new guest of honor pretty damn fast."

But O. J. returned and said he'd talked Jack Black into coming, after all. Everyone sighed gratefully, glad to be spared having to tolerate another one of Wayne Poe's dreadful performances.

"And now, gentlemen," said O. J., "my agenda is covered. Is there any other business to discuss? Yes, Al?"

Our Grand Sheik announced that he had a motion of vital importance to make.

"Yes? What is it?"

"RACK 'EM!"

Despite my headache, I had no intention of letting Butler slip away after the meeting. Considering his performance at the pool table and his totally out-of-character endorsement of Wayne Poe, I figured he was too sloshed to stand a chance against my own deck if we played gin.

For double insurance, I bought him a straight Bombay and Michelob chaser at the bar, then suggested riding over to West End Avenue for a rematch. He agreed and wanted to drive us there, but I hastily told him to leave the Packard in the Port Authority lot and let me treat us to a cab. It was a small price to pay for personal safety.

We walked over to Broadway and I stepped out in the street to flag down a taxi, but Butler tapped me on the shoulder. I turned. He was waving a couple of one-dollar bills in my face.

"Hey, boy, you got any quarters in change? This is important!"

I rooted in my pocket and found three quarters, a nickel and two dimes. He exchanged the coins for one of the dollars, told me to come along if I liked, and hurried up the block toward 43rd.

I followed, and saw him duck into Nathan's. I couldn't understand why he didn't just tell me he was hungry. But then, that didn't make sense, either . . . there was no reason why he needed quarters to buy a hot dog.

Opening the door of the raffish frankfurter emporium, I glanced around to locate Butler in the crowd. I saw him right up front, between the clam bar and the ice cream stand. He had both hands around a radar scanner, part of a kids' coin-play machine. His eyes were pressed to the visiplate, and he was gleefully demolishing enemy submarines.

"I saw this on the way over tonight," he told me when he'd blown up his final enemy vessel. "Figured it'd steady my eye for our game."

We didn't leave till he'd used up the other pair of quarters and bought a can of Schaefer's to "tranquilize" his nerves against the upcoming cab ride.

"You know what they say about New York City drivers, boy!"

In the taxi, I asked him why the sudden surge of admiration for Wayne Poe. He looked at me in astonishment.

"Are you loco? I'm gonna fry that bastard's ass!"

"How? By telling lies about how good he was?"

"Never mind," he said sullenly. "You just leave it up to the Old Man."

By way of informing Butler that I had no use for Poe, either, I said I'd never seen anything crummier than what Poe pulled on Bryan Harper, the young singer.

"He murdered the poor punk," Butler replied.

"You could say that."

"No, I mean, he *murdered* him!"

I looked sharply at Butler. His big face was grim. "What are you talking about, Old Man?" I asked, unconsciously adopting the label he regularly employed for himself.

"I mean, Poe killed that kid sure as if he'd shoved 'im under himself. Who do you think told the little dope to sing without the orchestra, instead of picking another number?"

"Yeah, but that's not—"

"And the combo got paid off by Poe, I checked. Y'know why?"

"Why?"

"Cliff Waxman was in the audience. Produces "Bright New Stars" for WCAU, big talent agent, too. Harper broke his nuts getting Waxman to come hear him (not that the kid was ready to be heard). But Poe sets the kid up, then sings the song himself with the band, and Cliff sees Poe afterwards and signs *him* for some rat's-ass cruise ship gig—right in front of Bryan! So junior gets the career-nipped-in-the-bud blues, goes out, gets sozzled, and steps off a curb in front of a truck—*whammo*! Instant gravy! Only thing didn't get twisted like a pretzel was some damn-fool good luck medal his uncle gave 'im. They fished it out of the pudding that was left on the street.''

"Jesus Christ," I murmured.

"*He* wasn't there," Butler snapped. "Unless you think singing' off-key's a good reason for Divine Zapping.''

We were silent the rest of the ride, mulling over Harper's fate.

Hilary controlled herself with considerable effort.

"He doesn't look all that drunk to me," she snapped.

"I am! I am!" Frank Butler assured her from his vantage point behind me.

"Trust me, he is," I told her in a low voice, "and don't you know a blow to the adam's apple could kill someone?"

It happened fast, practically as soon as Butler and I entered the apartment/office. Hilary went to shake his hand, but he gave her an affectionate pat on the bottom. The next thing I knew, he was scuttling behind me and the initial blow meant for Butler's neck landed on my own clavicle.

"Get out of the way!" she ordered, drawing back her hand for an intended karate chop in the general direction of the Old Man's gullet. I grabbed her hand with difficulty—she's petite, but strong as hell—and did my best to reason with her.

"Jeez, toots!" Butler said, over my shoulder. "I meant it as a compliment! If you were a dog, I wouldn't't've bothered!"

She stared at the two of us, speechless. I was positive his unique explanation would further incense her, and for a second I think Hilary thought so, too. Then the absurdity of the situation struck her and she exhaled a series of little gasps that sounded suspiciously like suppressed laughter.

"That," she remarked, "is the damnedest excuse I ever heard. Okay, you can come out from behind Daddy Gene's back, the Big Bad Broad won't hurt you."

Hilary asked how my collarbone felt. I said it hurt enough to convince me I wasn't cut out to be a masochist, but I was pretty sure it was still in one working piece.

"Glad to hear it, brightness. Now kindly tell me why you brought this old lech over here."

I pretended to explain, and she assumed the attitude of one who listens with polite interest. It was really a put-up performance for Butler's benefit. I'd told Hilary all about my Philadelphia escapades and she'd promised to watch our rematch to see whether she could catch him foxing the cards.

We adjourned to the sitting room-library where I'd left a new pack upon the tabletop where we were going to play. Butler walked ahead, and when he couldn't see us, Hilary shook her head in dismay.

"Saint preserve us," she muttered, her blue eyes glancing at the ceiling in mock appeal, "he has to be a detective yet!"

To Hilary, that was undoubtedly the unkindest cut of all.

The next hour and a quarter was devoted to gin rummy. We used a Bee-back deck, which I'd bought because of the eye-confusing red crisscross design which I'd heard was the hardest to mark impromptu.

Despite my precautions, Butler gained the lead after two hands and kept it practically straight through. My indebtedness mounted.

Hilary watched us silently as we played, perched on the edge of the sofa, her azure bathrobe comfortably wrapped around her tantalizing body. I pretended to myself that part of the reason I was not playing well was because the view of her legs distracted me more than it did Butler.

The Old Man had an uncanny knack of catching quick gins. He played in a loose, relaxed style, not squinting nervously over the cards he drew. The whole time we sat, he yakked about all manner of things, from his formidable relatives to the current status of the Two Tars tent. As he talked, he frequently lubricated his larynx with a swig from the fifth of gin stuck in his jacket pocket. At Hilary's request, he limited his cigar intake to two.

"Well, boy," he grinned after raking in his earnings at the end of the match, "you ready to admit the Old Man's a better player?"

"I still think you're pulling something. No offense." I've often wondered about people who say something inflammatory and then try to minimize it with the ridiculous phrase I'd just employed. But I meant it. I tried to convince Butler that I was more interested in learning how he'd flummoxed me than in achieving redress.

Nodding, Butler obtained Hilary's permission to light a third stogie. "Say, toots," he asked her, "you ain't got some walnuts in the house?" She shook her head. Shrugging, he muttered to himself, as if he couldn't comprehend a household lacking such a basic staple. "Well, now," he grumbled, puffing away, "y'want to know the Old Man's secrets, huh? Okay. I *will* admit I'm not as much in the bag as you figured. I don't mean just now, I'm talking about at The Lambs, too."

I considered it. "You mean, you *deliberately* blew the pool game just to make me overconfident?"

"Bingo, boy, you win the fur-lined jock-strap!" An anxious scowl contorted his homely features. "Hey, now, y' won't tell Kilgore, will you?"

"No. But I still don't know what you pulled. You did not read the card backs, I know that for a fact since we used my deck. I'm also positive you didn't manage anything fancy like dealing seconds or palming cards. Right?"

"Too much work," he grunted, exhaling the tantalizingly familiar aroma of his special brand of cigar in my direction. Then he reached into his vest pocket and yanked out an old-fashioned timepiece. "Tell you what, make you a sporting proposition. Give you five minutes to work it out, double or nothing the winnings."

"Does that offer include me, too?" Hilary asked, smiling ingenuously. Her innocent air was a credit to her early training as an actor.

"You?" Butler eyed her suspiciously. "What d'you know about gin rummy?" Before she could answer, he turned to me. "You two pulling some kind of swindle?"

"*Us?*" I laughed. "Who just named double stakes?"

"All right, you're in, cutie," the Old Man said, not too eagerly. "But the two of you can't talk it over. No conferences, see?"

"Agreed," Hilary replied, tossing her head so her hair glinted with highlights. "All I want is an opportunity to examine the cards with a magnifying glass."

Butler grinned. "Go right ahead!"

45

I started to tell her not to bother, but he repeated his stipulation about our not comparing notes. He looked craftily pleased with the situation. No wonder.

"I warn you, Mr. Butler," Hilary taunted, "I have very keen eyes."

"I'll say, toots!"

"Thank you. I don't suppose you'd care to up the ante, double stakes either way?"

The old pirate probably wanted to hike the bet to a triple multiple, but he pretended to mull over her challenge. I knew he was totally confident, despite the act he was putting on. She could study the deck with a magnifier or even a microscope, it didn't matter, there wasn't the remotest chance she'd learn anything from a card-by-card scrutiny of a brand-new pack. He knew it, I knew it, and I didn't know why the hell she didn't.

Finally, he ventured to take the "risk," double stakes. Hilary rose, cards in hand, and went to the front office for her magnifying lens. Butler grinned at me a little sheepishly. He must have been a bit ashamed to accept such a sure thing.

Hilary reentered, apologizing for the delay. "I couldn't find the damn thing," she said, holding up the enlarger.

"It's okay," said Butler, "but you already used up two minutes."

Without another word, she sat down and studied the back markings of each and every card, pausing scarcely more than a second before going on to the next. She totally ignored the faces.

Butler sat watching the second hand of his Bulova sweep away the dwindling time. At the end of five minutes, he stuck the watch back in his vest pocket and asked her what she'd found out, if anything. He sounded pleased with himself.

"But how will I know if I'm right?" she challenged him. "All we'll have will be *your* word."

She let the heavy-footed implication dangle.

"Okay," Butler said smugly, "you go outta the room and I'll tell Gene here what I did, and he'll judge whether you come anywhere close. Copacetic?"

"All right," Hilary agreed.

She left the room long enough for Butler to explain his

system. When I heard, I felt stupid for not getting it, but I'd been too busy pondering more complicated methods. I was only sorry that Hilary was about to blow her money on some hyper-subtle hypothesis.

We called her back into the library. She took the cards and began idly shuffling them as she spoke.

"Gin," she said, "is a game in which both players start with ten cards in their hands. The winner of each round deals the next hand. Those are important facts. As for clues—the way you shuffled tended to leave the top cards undisturbed. Second, from one hand to another, there was an unusual recurrence of similar meld sequences when you called gin."

Butler began to look worried.

"As dealer, all you have to do is assemble some of those melds on the table as consecutive, undisturbed packets and make sure they go on top of the deck. Then you take care to riffle-shuffle so they fall in a heap at the end of the mixing. It's so easy and natural to do that no one can call it cheating."

"Anything else?" Butler growled.

"Oh, yes. All you need to do to get those winning melds where you want them is to pass the cards to Gene to be cut. Card custom is not to cut less than ten cards, and as a matter of fact, most people divide the deck in half. I imagine you remember the top card of your first undisturbed meld and watch for that one to be turned up in the course of play. When you see it, you start picking up every single card you can lay your hands on—top of the talon, your opponent's discards. *He* sure can't use the cards that are turning over to improve his hand, while all the time you're just trading your initial cards for the sequenced ones you've stacked in the middle." Pausing, she raised one eyebrow and regarded him with sardonic amusement. "Well, am I right, or am I right?"

He grimaced, but said nothing, so she turned to me. I nodded. "You've got it, Hilary. The only difference is he memorizes the top *two* cards of the middle melds, just in case the other player draws the first and doesn't discard it."

Butler was silent for a time, then, turning to Hilary, stuck a fat finger in her direction. "How come you went through all that crap about examining the cards with a magnifier?"

47

"I believe," she said, smiling icily, "that's what's known as setting up the mark. I wanted you to take my double-stakes bet."

I thought Butler would utter a few choice imprecations, but he surprised me by grinning and passing his bottle to Hilary.

"You're okay, blondie! Here—have some firewater!"

She took it, too—though Hilary doesn't like liquor unless it's iced or watered or mixed. But she downed a good two and a half ounces. The improvident helping of gin brought on a coughing fit, followed by an attack of the giggles, a decidedly uncharacteristic phenomenon for Hilary. I felt embarrassed for her.

We sat and talked for a while, and Hilary held onto Butler's bottle, taking a few more swigs. She grew decidedly tipsy.

"I've got an idea," she said, after several minutes. Her voice was somewhat thick, as if her tongue was too big for her mouth. "How about—Gene, what do you call it? You know, when you decide you're going to keep your money in the pot?"

"What? Letting it ride?"

"That's it." She turned to Butler. "How about it? Y'wanna let it ride?"

"I don't get you." He stubbed out his cigar. "You saying we should play gin honest-like?" The idea seemed to appall him.

"Not gin," she replied. "Bridge."

"*Bridge*?" He stared at her as if she were screwy.

"Hilary," I politely reminded her, "it takes four to play bridge."

"No-no," she argued, speech slurring. "One player always sits out." Her eyes looked crossed.

Her idea was nutty. In bridge, the first thing that happens in every hand is that the two competing teams bid for the privilege of naming trumps. The winners have to take in a number of tricks determined by the size of the bid with which they won the auction. During the bidding, neither partner may look at the other's hand, though afterwards, one member of the team sits out and lays his cards face-up on the table for his partner to play (and his opponents to see). This face-up hand is called the dummy. Hilary wanted to automatically accept the obligation of winning a certain number of tricks, playing both her hand and the dummy—even though there are many times in bridge when such poor cards are received that it's wise to avoid winning the contract and setting trumps. If Butler took her bet, she would be totally at the mercy of the deal.

I said all this to her, then added that there was something else wrong with the idea. "If you automatically accept the contract, Hilary, would you tell me how in hell you are going to know how many tricks to set and what suit to call as trumps if you're not permitted to examine your 'partner's hand' at that point?"

"Easy," she shrugged. "I'll announce my contract on the sole basis of the cards I have in my own hand."

Which was sheer, stupid madness!

The avarice was growing in the Old Man's eyes. He didn't have to be asked twice whether he wanted to play. It was unfair to take advantage of her in the condition she was in, and I was extremely reluctant to be a party to the proceedings, but she insisted that I take the east hand.

"What're the stakes?" Butler asked. I swear his voice trembled.

"You name them," said Hilary, punctuating her remark with a hiccup.

It must have been hard for Butler to reconcile his warring senses of avarice and compassion. But he may have remembered that Hilary queered his gin game inasmuch as he finally suggested a bet that was little short of indecent.

And Hilary, the damn fool, took it.

She began to shuffle the cards, but her reflexes were an uncoordinated mess and she made a lousy job of it. Cards went all over the tabletop. She gathered them, mixed them as best she could, then embarked upon the strangest travesty of a bridge deal that I've ever witnessed. Her trouble was that her brain was too muddled for her to count correctly. First she dealt three cards to Butler, then one to the dummy, four to me and five to herself. Shaking her head, she deposited two from her hand onto the dummy, then took one away from me and gave it to the Old Man. But still that wasn't right, so she had to distribute more cards to even it out, only she miscounted again. I tried to give her a little help, but she slapped my hand away.

"I can do it," she protested, "I'll show you!" Hilary waved me off with a gesture so flamboyant she nearly fell off her chair.

Well, somehow or other she actually managed to distribute the cards. It took much arbitrary fishing of haphazard pasteboards from one place to another, but at last there were thirteen cards in every hand.

"That's the sloppiest deal I ever saw," Butler complained.

I sighed and picked up my hand to sort it into suits. Right away, I noticed I had a void in spades.

"My contract," said Hilary Quayle, "is seven spades."

Had I been eating, I would've gagged. She'd named one of the highest bids and hardest contracts to fill in all bridge. To make it, she'd have to win all thirteen tricks, a near impossibility.

Butler guffawed loud and long. "Talk about dumb broads! Seven spades! Chrissake, you'd better have practically every—"

He shut up and stared. So did I.

Hilary was no longer slouching in her seat. A moment earlier, her eyes had been valiantly trying to focus, but now they shone with a cold, mocking light. One by one, she turned over her cards so we could see them.

She had a trump grand slam—every single spade from the ace through the king.

"I think," she understated, "this is what is known as an unbeatable combination, *n'est-ce pas?*"

I didn't know the exact odds, but I was pretty sure it would be easier to get a royal flush in poker on the initial deal, without drawing.

"So," I said, "you aren't drunk after all."

"If you'd thought I was sober, would either of you have tolerated that outrageous deal?"

"What the hell's going on?" Butler demanded.

"Remember when I went out to get my magnifying glass?" she asked. "In case you don't recall, I took the cards with me. When I was alone, I removed the spades and put them on top of the pack."

"Yeah, but I saw you shuffle 'em later."

"Not till I'd examined them, one at a time. During the process, it was simple for me to bend the corners of each spade a

50

little, just enough so they would be easy to recognize when I dealt like a drunk.''

"Goddamn!'' Butler swore. ''Conned twice. I feel like the guy in Aesop whose donkey keeps kicking him and he says, 'Once more unto the breach!' ''

She pointed a finger at him. ''In case you wonder what you did to deserve two knuckle-raps, you can write off the gin rummy business as a favor to Gene. But conning you at bridge is my way of paying you back for getting fresh.''

''I thought we were square on that!''

''Only when I thought you were drunk.''

He glowered at her, probably wondering whether to admire her chutzpah or kick her in the pants—a reaction to Hilary with which I was extremely familiar.

The Old Man left ten minutes later. He would have stomped out immediately, but I slipped past and blocked the door until he decided to pay up.

CUT TO:

Medium shot. The Lambs. Early June.

Since it was the Friday of the New York banquet, I received special dispensation from Hilary to take the day off and help the special events committee decorate and set up.

I should have known better than to come on time, but it was a bright, sunny morning, so I didn't mind the prospect of waiting ten or fifteen minutes outside the entrance of the club for the rest of the volunteers to arrive.

Optimist that I was, I showed up at five after nine. No one else appeared till way past ten. By then, I'd grown tired of waiting underneath the blue awning, so I grabbed a seat in the lounge and started reading Jack McCabe's *The Comedy World of Stan Laurel*, which I'd brought along to occupy myself during the bus ride over.

The earliest of the latecomers was our treasurer, Natie Barrows, he of the eternally nervous smile and Mary Tyler Moore T-shirt.

We said hello. He was agitated. I asked him what was wrong.

"Did you hear what O. J. pulled? I just found out!"

"What?"

"Wayne Poe's on the show tonight!"

"Doesn't surprise me."

A new voice sounded. *"He's got who on the show?"*

We turned. The speaker was Barry Richmond. He looked shocked.

Natie repeated his news. Barry shook his head.

"You'd think," he said, "O. J. would learn from experience. He asked Poe to do ten minutes last year, and he bored the hell out of everybody for half an hour."

52

"Not only that," Natie said, his voice trembling with indignation, "but Poe did the same material then that we heard two years before."

The door opened and O. J. walked in. He was instantly pounced on.

"I don't understand what you're objecting to," he said evenly, his innocent blue eyes widening. "Last year, when Jody Lange got sick at the last minute, Wayne did me a big favor and filled in. He's been a real friend to the Sons, and Frank Butler says Wayne got a great big hand in Philly. I'm asking him to do just ten minutes right after the skit. Frank suggested that, too."

"Since when," Natie demanded, "does a Two Tars officer decide parent tent business?"

"Don't be so huffy," O. J. admonished him. "All Frank did was make a suggestion. I was on the telephone with him yesterday because I needed the dates of the Philly-New York confab to announce at dinner tonight . . . otherwise, no one's going to be there. So while we were talking, Frank asked if Poe was going to be on the banquet show and I said yes, then mentioned I was wondering who to put on after the skit. Sandy's too green to follow a show-stopper. So that's when Butler said I ought to use a professional in that spot, and he urged me to pick Poe."

Butler said he wanted to murder Poe, and he meant it. The skit featured Jack Black in his first live appearance in a decade and a half. The nostalgia quotient alone would bring down the house, and I pitied any poor slob who had to try to top it. The sensible decision would have been to schedule a musical number afterwards, but O. J.'s forte is selling hats, not routining entertainment.

It was no use bickering with O. J. He couldn't be riled, he just smiled and talked around any and every complaint and ended up doing what he wanted, anyway. Natie gave up and let Barry have the floor. His Excellency ran through a fair-sized itinerary of last-minute things that needed to be done.

For the next three hours, I helped hang streamers, rooted in dusty storage closets on the third floor of The Lambs for electrical cable and connectors, and mounted dozens of stills from Laurel and Hardy films. I made a trip to get the programs, an extra projection lamp, and miscellaneous push-pins, luminous tape, Coca-Colas, and beer.

By one o'clock, it was time to accompany O. J. on the upstate drive to the AGVA home.

It took about an hour to get there. Jack Black, waiting for us at the front desk, was nattily dressed and carried a small valise. He suggested we stop in for a moment to say hello to his ailing friend and ex-partner.

Billy White was sitting up in bed when we entered. His body had not suffered the whittling influence of time nearly so much as Black's. There was still a lot of flesh on his frame, though much of it hung in loose folds. He was nearly bald, and his jowls, stubbled with whiskers, were unhealthy in color.

"Good to see you, O. J.," he wheezed in a frail, breathy tenor that sounded like a man who'd been walking too long and hard. His mouth was curiously slack and it was not easy to understand what he was saying. Black explained in a low voice that White's stroke had nearly paralyzed the entire right side of his face, though it had evidently not impaired his thinking.

I can't reproduce the exact sound, but it took all his will to shape the words which we had to strain for.

"Sorry I can't come with Jackie," he laboriously told O. J. "Gotta stay in bed. Give my love to Hal." He coughed. Even that was an effort. Feebly, he pressed O. J.'s hands in his gnarled fingers.

On our way out, O. J. told me that White is Hal Fawkes's uncle. "That's how we got them to agree to be our banquet guests." He turned to Jack Black and asked what caused White's stroke.

"He got some bad news," Black replied. "Couldn't take it."

The nonagenarian walked briskly, setting a difficult pace. Age had not hampered him much; he was still tough. Slight and wiry, Black had a head shaped like an egg, the point being his chin. His big eyes were comically grotesque behind thick bifocals he wore attached to a cord. He was a fine choice for Fin, even to the high forehead, though Black lacked a mustache. All

54

in all, he resembled a cross between an elegant undertaker and Charlie McCarthy.

I offered to take his bag to the car, but he shook me off.

"I was on the road seventy years," he said in his crisp, incisive voice. "No porter ever touched *my* bags." I could sympathize with his pride: at his age every victory against the rigors of encroaching Time must be reassuring. Nevertheless, after pitching the valise into the trunk of O. J.'s red Maverick, he settled into the rear seat with a very audible sigh.

It was a little before four P.M. when we pulled up in front of The Lambs. I got out first and helped Black clamber onto the sidewalk. O. J. took the old man's bag from the trunk, gave it to him, then drove away to park in a garage up the street.

We were barely on time. The skit was supposed to rehearse at four, and since it would be the only time the rest of the cast could do it with Black, I expected that (contrary to usual Sons custom), the rehearsal would get underway on the dot.

I was right. Everyone was waiting for us in the third-floor Lambs theater. Tye Morrow, our tent's ex-president, was directing; he sat in the front row going over last-minute notes with Natie, who'd exchanged his MTM T-shirt for a costume and makeup that made him look like Oliver Hardy.

Onstage, the diffident delegate, Toby Sanders, waited in Stan Laurel garb and gear. He was talking to O. J.'s wife, Della, who was made up like Mae Busch. Della was full-bosomed and tall, with honey-blonde hair that demanded only minimal aid from Clairol. She was always either laughing or smiling, much of the time at the supposed witticisms of the omnipresent gents then dancing attendance on her. Most of the men in the tent dearly lusted after her.

She was always worth a second look, but this time I had to give her a third. The premise of the skit was "Laurel and Hardy in the Garden of Eden," but Toby and Natie's garb was standard: suits and ties and bowlers; the only concession to Biblical tradition was a feeble attempt to twine ivy about their skypieces. Della, on the other hand, had not been permitted nearly so liberal an interpretation of costuming in her role of Lilith. She was showing more skin than I'd ever been privileged to scan, and I couldn't deny being appreciative of the chance.

55

Black took a few minutes to get into makeup and costume as "the landlord" of the Garden of Eden. He pulled on a baldhead rubber skullpiece, affixed bushy eyebrows and mustache, and transformed himself into a tolerable look-alike of Jimmy Finlayson. Tye leaned over and flicked on a tape recorder in the empty orchestra pit, and the run-through began.

I was halfway up the aisle, ready to leave, but I couldn't resist watching the old trouper in his first performance onstage in a good fifteen years. "The Cuckoo Song" played and Adam (Ollie/Natie) and Eve (Stan/Toby) walked on. They approached the sole piece of stage scenery, a large, two-dimensional apple tree. After a bit of pantomimic by-play, Ollie pushed a finger against a knothole in the tree unit and a doorbell rang, followed by a heavenly fanfare.

Jack Black entered, twirling his phony mustache. Despite his ninety-plus years, he did a little ridiculous hop-skip that looked exactly like the one Stan performed whenever he saw an attractive woman in the short comedy "Putting Pants on Philip." Everyone from Tye through the rest of the cast cracked up when he did it, and Black looked pleased, though he didn't break out of character.

"That bitch-mother! Goddamn it!"

I swung around, amazed at the vehemence of the imprecation. It had not been uttered loudly, and I doubted that anyone heard it but me.

In the back of the theater stood Wayne Poe, his chilly professional smile plastered on his face in a ghastly parody of mirth. There was a woman standing next to him. She started to whisper something to him, but Poe turned abruptly on his heel and marched out of the theater.

I approached the other. It was Sandy Sable, a thirtyish mousy brunette who barely measured up to the middle of my chest. She was the protégée of the parent tent, a clever monologist whose area of specialization was nostalgic humor. Onstage she was vivacious and wistfully appealing at the same time, but when she wasn't performing, she retired inside herself and took most of her personality with her.

The only times I'd seen her before were when she was doing her comedy act and on those occasions she was always smartly dressed. But O. J. said she never took that wardrobe onto the street for fear of losing the full tax credits she deducted for clothing. So there, in the darkened rear of The Lambs' theater, Sandy blended into the woodwork in a tattered white short-sleeved blouse and faded jeans she couldn't do justice to.

"What was wrong with him?" I asked her, jerking my thumb in Poe's direction.

The ghost of a smile twitched her lips, but immediately disappeared. "He just learned he has to go on after the play. Isn't that a shame?" She stared up at me with large watery brown eyes. "Do you know me?" she asked shyly, inverting the usual form of the question to suit her comedian's need for recognition.

"Sure. You're Sandy Sable."

Her smile lasted a fraction of a second longer this time. "What's your name?"

"Gene."

"Gene, would you do me a very special favor?" She asked it in such a low voice that for a second I thought it was going to be something very personal. Somewhere in the depths of her eyes I sensed an individual I would like to get to know.

I asked her what the favor was and she beckoned me to follow her. She walked to the left side of the theater house, opened a door in the rear wall and passed through. I wondered what the hell I was getting into, but I followed.

We were in a small dark room filled by a long walnut conference table, chairs, and bookshelves crammed full of ancient plays and books of theatrical theory and history. She flicked on the light and asked me to take a seat.

For the next half-hour, Sandy Sable tried out every bit of new comedy material she'd written over the past three months. After each punch line, I had to tell her whether I *really* thought the joke was funny, or if I was just laughing to be polite, because I felt I had to. Actually, she would have been surprised how low my store of politeness had waned by the time I extricated myself from her flypaper grasp.

She'd made me late, and I had to hurry home to change and pick up Hilary. I was still tiptoeing around the office to spare her any added aggravation. One of our accounts, Trim-Tram Toys, had just canceled its contract and we were in rocky financial shape, a condition in no way ameliorated by Uncle Sam's magnetic affinity for our income.

I had an awful feeling Hilary was going to find out about the parent tent's stag membership policy that evening, and I fully expected the night to end in emotional fireworks.

But things started off much more smoothly than I'd thought possible. She was already dressed when I got back to the apartment, and I nodded approval at the alluring green silk pants suit and simple matching jacket. Her hair was in an upsweep, a style I'd never seen her wear before. Usually, Hilary either let her hair hang loose about her shoulders or tied it severely in back.

"How do you like it?" she smiled, indicating the hairdo with a graceful upward movement of both arms.

"I wouldn't have said it was you, but it looks great!"

"Tonight, it *is* me," she said, taking my arm. "Gene, I've been looking forward to this evening. If there's something I can really use today, it's a good laugh."

I agreed, but added I could also use a drink. Now Hilary is stubborn, she insists on chipping in half on the cost of our dates. Since I knew she was worried about money, I suggested a cocktail beforehand at Beefsteak Charlie's, one of the more satisfying economical restaurant chains in the city. Considering the usual open-bar prices one finds at banquets, I figured Charlie's would be easier on her purse.

By the time we got to The Lambs, the cocktail hour was well under way, and so were we. Negotiating the stairs carefully, we entered the second-floor lounge, where the welcoming committee greeted us—O. J., Hal Fawkes, and Al Kilgore. Hal and O. J. checked us off on the master list and fished out identification badges which Kilgore inscribed with our names.

"Howya, honey," he said to Hilary, "Gene tells us all about ya!" He gestured jauntily. "I'd slap 'im, if I were you."

Hilary was tipsy enough not to care what I might have said about her in her absence. She laughed it off, put on her badge, and took my arm as we began a circuit of the lounge to the opposite side where the bar and, therefore, most of the activity was.

58

It was a big rectangular place with two arms, too small to be considered wings, stretching toward 44th Street. Deep, luxurious beige carpeting covered every inch of the flooring and there were immense oil paintings of Kean, Booth, Beerbohn-Tree, and other bygone thespians suspended all about the room. Twenty linen-covered dining tables covered most of the area. The head table, mounted on a dais, stretched the width of the room. A huge blow-up poster of Al Kilgore's escutcheon rested in front of it, while behind, on the wall, there was a big movie screen, not yet pulled down.

On the side of the room opposite from where we entered, an alcove provides access to a second staircase running both up and down, to the men's rest room, and a door into the second-floor kitchen. At the moment, the area of the alcove was the scene of considerable bustling of Lambs waiters and cooks.

As we headed for the bar, Hilary commented on the small, attractive platform stage Barry had constructed to the left of the dais. Though there was the theater on the floor above, it was too big for intimate cabaret entertainment, so Barry spent a healthy chunk of Sons capital to provide a stylish place for the performers of the evening: a proscenium draped in the club colors, blue and white, with stills from Laurel and Hardy films adorning the uprights.

The extreme left edge of the stage abutted the wall. Steps led down from the platform and out of sight to the far door of the kitchen, which later on would be used as "wings" for performers to wait in before going onstage.

On our way over to the bar, we had to pass right by the door to the second staircase. As we did, I noticed a man slinking stealthily upstairs. As he neared the open door to the banquet hall, he ducked his head, hurried past, and continued on his way to the third floor, where the dressing rooms were located.

I wondered why Dutchy Hovis was acting like a fugitive. Whom was he hoping to avoid?

A large crowd of people thronged the ell in which the bar was situated. Men in white jackets, leisure suits, blazers embroidered with Sons of the Desert escutcheons, milled around the lineless service counter and vied for the bartender's attention. Women in slacks, evening gowns, tailored suits, and here and there a simple skirt-blouse combo, laughed and chatted with one another or whichever guest they cared to flatter. Wayne Poe was in the middle of the group, talking louder than anyone. I had to walk by his coterie to get to the bar; he was holding forth on the trials of putting on a network TV series. I shuddered; it would be too much to hope that O. J. hadn't run down film clips of Poe's turkey of a program.

Toby called me over and introduced me to Rosina Lawrence, the heroine of Laurel and Hardy's feature *Way Out West*. One zealous tent member tracked her down after her whereabouts had been unknown for years. Ironically, she lived not far from Manhattan. Her delicate features and winsome smile were little changed since the year the film was released, 1937.

Hilary took the Gibson from me and we ambled about, saying hello to various members of the Sons I wanted her to meet. Nearby, I saw Natie talking to Bob and Ray. I heard Bob Elliott asking, with great gravity, whether the dulcimers had been purchased as he'd stipulated.

"You know we can't do any of our material without the dulcimers," he warned Natie, who was doing his valiant best to keep a straight face.

Ray Goulding chimed in. "I think I saw the crate of monkeys downstairs. I hope they sent all six."

Barry Richmond tapped me on the shoulder. He had his usual Coke in his hand and looked deservedly exhausted.

"Hilary," I said, "meet His Excellency Sir Barry Alan Richmond—"

Before I could finish, she was in the midst of a curtsey. "Your honor," she said deferentially, "your fame precedes you!" She rose, cocked an eyebrow, and demanded that Barry tell us what was being done for women's equality in Montmartre.

"As a matter of fact, that's a very important issue," Barry replied glibly, "and I just enacted an edict that all female citizens have to wear a government-issue standard one-size bra. The next step will be to make them all equal in height. We've got a Japanese Secretary of the Exterior, but his plan to extend foot-binding from the soles of the feet to the top of the head is definitely not going to *last*. Get it?"

"Got it."

"Good."

"Speaking of length," he went on unflagging, "did I ever mention how long the Montmartre year is?"

Hilary shook her head. "You couldn't have. We just met."

"No, I don't mean did I ever mention it to you, but did I ever mention it at all?"

She laughed, defeated. "I don't know, Mr. Tambo, but tell me, how long *is* the Montmartre year?"

"It's a problem," Barry admitted, adjusting his glasses, "because it's only 365 days long, not 365 and a quarter. So every Leap Year we lose a day!"

Hilary drained her glass in one swallow and headed back to the bar for a much-needed refill. Barry sometimes has that effect.

Suddenly, everything went dark. At the front of the room, there was a noise: Hal pulling down the movie screen. A bright light played on it and became the image of Oliver Hardy, dressed elegantly, beaming at the camera. He told us with great self-importance that dinner was ready, "everything from soup to nuts." In this way, the Sons informed everyone that The Lambs dining staff was about to serve dinner.

The room rocked with laughter, the lights came back on, and there was a general move toward the tables. Hilary took my arm, not so much out of affection as a need for an anchor, and we went to the place designated on our identification badges.

Each table held ten settings, but only nine people were seated at ours. The woman beside me was next to the empty chair. During introductions, I learned her name was Isabel Hovis, Dutchy's wife.

"He's going to be late, he had to work overtime," she told us as she tried to smile. But the expression was unsuccessful because she had too many lines on her face headed in the opposite direction.

"We're used to Dutchy arriving late," Natie Barrows remarked.

She shrugged her narrow shoulders. "So am I."

No more was said about our absent member, but I wondered why he didn't want his wife to know he was already there.

Phil Faxon was one of the other people at our table. I heard him grumbling to Natie about Wayne Poe, who was seated on the dais with the other guests.

"I give him his start, that louse, y'know that?"

Natie shook his head, pretending to be ignorant of the fact.

"Why, sure," Phil said. "I used to be an agent, once upon a time, didn'tcha know?" He lowered his voice an octave, so that he sounded like Tony Marvin, Arthur Godfrey's radio announcer. "Phil Faxon, young man-about-town, impresario, agent, and producer." He changed back to his natural tone. "I discovered Wayne Poe. Lot of good it ever did me, what he pulled, almost got my head blown off."

Natie feigned surprise, made interested sounds, and let Phil ramble. Everybody on the executive committee had frequently heard how Poe had embroiled Phil Faxon with gangsters a good fifteen years before, but it was not considered gentlemanly to call Phil on his eternal repetitions. What else did the poor old coot have to talk about?

Despite the fact that the Sons constitution states that all officers must sit at the head table, it is rarely done. That night, O. J., in the seat farthest left and closest to Barry's platform stage, wisely occupied the place next to Wayne Poe, thus reducing potential dais friction 50 percent. On Poe's left, Jack Black ate slowly and occasionally addressed a remark to his neighbor, Rosina Lawrence. Ray Goulding also chatted with her, while his partner, Bob, engaged in conversation with Sons co-founder Chuck McCann, resplendent in a shiny summer-weight gold blazer. Rodney Dangerfield had the next chair; beyond him, Butterfly McQueen—who hadn't aged much since *Gone With the Wind*—picked at the salad she'd ordered instead of the prime ribs she, a vegetarian, could not eat. Every so often, she glanced up, smiling shyly, at some question or remark made by Grand Sheik Al Kilgore, seated on the extreme right of the banquet's head table.

The waiters began to pour the coffee. O. J. rose and rapped his water glass with a spoon. Though the banquet was by no means formal, our president had on a modern-cut tuxedo with tartan cummerbund and a ruffled-front-and-cuffs white shirt.

"Would Marty Kondak and Barry Richmond please come to the dais?" O. J. asked. It took a minute for them to get there—Barry had to be hunted down upstairs where he was doing some last-minute thing with a spotlight. When they both mounted the dais, Al Kilgore and Jack Black rose and joined them.

At O. J.'s request, everyone stood up and held their various libations aloft.

"The toast to Mae Busch and Charley Hall," O. J. announced, "will be delivered by His Honor Barry Richmond."

"Not Hizzoner," Barry protested, "My Excellency!"

"Barry," O. J. pleaded, "do the toast."

"Eh bien," Barry said, raising his glass of Coke. "A Charles et Mae, deux drôles magnifiques!' He took a sip, then added, "That's what you call a French toast."

A hearty groan, and the cry of "Hear, hear!" signified the general drinking of the pledge.

O. J. leaned in to the microphone. "The toast to Fin will be given by Marty Kondak."

A slim, tall man in navy-blue nautical jacket stepped forward. He had a pencil-thin mustache and wore glasses. This was the uncrowned "Poet Lariat" of the parent tent, Marty Kondak, whose specialty was toasts in rhyme. Drawing a piece of notepaper from his pocket, he found the appropriate bit of poesy and sang a paean to Jimmy Finlayson to the tune of "M-O-T-H-E-R."

> "F is for the frowns he always gave them,
> I is for the icy stare he had.
> N is for the nasty tricks he played them,
> For he was good at being very bad.

L is for the leers that—A—were awful.
Y is for the yelling and the yowls
As he duped the boys with schemes unlawful
And squints and sneers and sniggers, sniffs and scowls.
S-O-N, you know what kind I'm meaning,
A finer heavy there has never been!
You see the way my final rhyme is leaning:
Here's to our Jimmy—F-I-N—TO FIN!''

"Hear, Hear!" the company proclaimed, once more raising glasses high.

Al Kilgore delivered Babe's toast. "Once, Jack McCabe asked Stan how come he always seemed to watch Babe whenever looking at one of their films. Stan's answer was simple—'He really is a funny, funny fellow.' Well, here's to Babe, a man who could make *Stan* laugh!"

"*Hear, hear!*"

"Last but certainly not least," said O. J., "the toast to Stan will be given by our special guest of honor, Mr. Jack Black."

If we hadn't already been standing, we would have all gotten up then. The applause rang out loud and long.

Black shook his head as O. J. invited him to step up to the microphone. He stayed where he was. "Pardon me if I avoid that electric crutch. When Billy and I started out, there was no such thing on a stage as a mike. We had to know how to project straight to the last row of the house. It's practically a lost art." He sipped his drink and continued. "A toast to Stan, yes . . . a privilege. A solemn duty. Comedy is a great art. I have devoted my life to it. My religion has no hymns, only laughter. If top bananas are the high priests of my church, then Stan Laurel was a goddamned cardinal!"

"HEAR, HEAR!"

Everyone cheered. O. J. patted the old trouper on the back.

After we were seated, Al Kilgore read telegrams from friends and absentee members, then O. J. got up and announced the date of the Philadelphia-New York joint convention, which was to be held less than one month later.

"Considering the brevity of time to prepare," O. J. said, "we'd like to find out if anyone contemplates going."

There was a good show of hands. It occurred to me that I

hadn't seen Frank Butler all evening, but I was sure he meant to attend.

"Wonder where the old buzzard is," I said to Hilary.

"Who knows? Maybe his Packard died in the swamps of New Jersey."

Butler didn't show until the dais portion of the banquet was nearly over. By then, Dangerfield had done a few, too few, hilarious minutes, and Chuck performed a pantomime based on the idea that Bob Cummings's eternal youthfulness might be the result of fantastically intricate prosthetic devices. Bob and Ray did their classic interview with the cranberry grower and the chat with the Komodo Dragon authority. Then Ray reached down and accepted the plaque which Mel Fawkes had nearly broken as he tripped carrying it to the dais. As prior recipients of the Sons comedy achievement award, the team had agreed to present the current one to Jack Black.

The old man made a few gracious remarks on behalf of himself and the absent Billy White. When he was done, Natie mounted the dais and began calling off numbers for the annual auction. Just then, I saw a large figure in a white suit enter at the back of the room. It was Frank Butler. He was carrying a big package wrapped in brown paper, treating it delicately.

"Who ever told him he should wear white?" Hilary said. "He looks like a pregnant light bulb."

Butler saw us and approached. "Hey, boy, how the hell you doin'?" He pumped my hand in his free mitt, started to reach over to Hilary, thought better of it and yanked his hand back.

"Where've you been?" I asked. "The meal's already over."

"It's all right, I ate on the road. Hadda chase all over Philly to find exactly what I wanted."

He patted the package.

"What's inside?"

"Shh." Butler shook his head. "You'll see." Chuckling, he waddled off in the direction of the head table.

During the break while they were rearranging the seats for the platform show, Hilary told me she was enjoying herself and wanted to join the Sons of the Desert.

I ignored the statement. "Hilary," I said, "you've *got* to see the club's library. They've got a limited edition of Percy Mackaye's *Hamlet*."

That was enough to divert her. It was a book she'd been vainly trying to acquire for the better part of a decade. I took her to the trophy room/library in the recess beyond the bar. When she saw the huge boxed Bond Wheelwright tome, she gasped, delighted.

"I didn't know it would be so *big*! May I look at it, hold it?" A little girl anxious to play with someone else's toys.

I waved to Hal, who was running around passing out bar chits to guests. "Is it all right to handle the books, Hal?"

"As long as you don't get 'em dirty and put 'em back." He zoomed off on another errand, narrowly avoiding a belly-whop when his toe snagged the cord of an electric wire.

"That," said Hilary, "is the clumsiest man I ever met."

I agreed.

For the next few minutes, Hilary occupied herself caressing the rare book. I wasn't so sure I should have distracted her. I knew damn well it'd be worse for me, the longer I delayed telling her she couldn't join the Sons.

"*Take your seats. The show's about to start.*"

The tables were pushed aside, and the chairs, arranged in neat rows, commanded both stage and the screen behind the dais. Ushers drafted from the general membership passed out programs.

There were nine items listed on the itinerary, starting with a "magic lantern show" and a "surprise" by Hal Fawkes and continuing through the skit, Wayne Poe, a singer, a magician, Sandy Sable's comedy act, and, next to last, Al Kilgore doing a couple of music-hall songs in honor of Stan's early days on the London variety circuit. The final thing, as always, was to be a Laurel and Hardy film, this time, as O. J. had told us, *The Hoose-Gow*.

I took a seat on the aisle and saved the next place for Hilary, who was not quite finished admiring The Lambs' library. She missed the opening greetings of the master of ceremonies, Phil Faxon.

I was interested to see that O. J. had found an innocuous way to give Phil something to do.

The lights went out and the "magic lantern show" began. It consisted of slides and film clips that introduced the boys and the guests of the evening. Excerpts from "The Tonight Show" spotlighted Rodney Dangerfield and Bob and Ray, and there were brief excerpts from *The Heart Is a Lonely Hunter* and *Gone With the Wind* in honor of Chuck McCann and Butterfly McQueen.

"The next thing you will see," Hal's voice said over the microphone, "is the only remaining footage of *The Knifethrower* starring our own Mae Busch."

There was an appreciative murmur from the members who knew their film history.

"*The Knifethrower*," Hal explained, "is generally considered a lost comedy, one of the first that Mae appeared in for the Famous-Kennett Studios. To the best of my knowledge, this incomplete segment is all that still exists of what was probably a two-reeler. The music you'll hear was put on magnetically when the original was transferred to more permanent stock."

The screen flickered to life. It was hard to make out the image. Mae, looking as white as Carl Dreyer's vampire, sauntered out onto the platform of a carnival stage wearing spangly briefs, the costume of a showgirl. A tall man with a long bristly mustache stood glowering at her, knives in hand.

"In the missing opening reel," Hal said, "the knifethrower sees his wife, played by Mae, fooling around with Elmer Parrott, the comedy star of the flick."

67

Mae wiggled her way to the bull's-eye target, evidently oblivious to the fact that her mate contemplated murder.

CUT TO: shot of Elmer Parrott, his goggle-eyes wider than ever, as Mae's maid whispered in his ear. I gathered she was telling him the awful truth.

CUT TO: the carnival sideshow. The crowd watched eagerly as a small boy walked onstage and stood beside the knife-thrower. The child took the knives and held them while the showman limbered up. Mae laughed at the ridiculous spectacle when he bent his bandy legs.

CLOSE-UP: the knife-thrower glowered straight into the camera.

CUT TO: Elmer Parrott hopping onto his bicycle to hurry to the carnival. The front wheel fell off.

The knife-thrower selected a dagger from the boy, aimed it—

"Now watch this," Hal said. "He actually throws the knife. The camera doesn't cut away!"

It was a medium shot, enough to contain Mae and the back of the male actor. Z-z-zip—the knife whizzed across the intervening space to imbed itself forcefully in the target scant inches from Mae's head.

CLOSE-UP: Startled expression on Mae's face.

And back to Elmer Parrott, riding a giddily tilted bike on the back wheel only. Needless to say, he arrived in time to save his beloved—only to see her make up with hubby at the fade out.

There was a round of applause when the tantalizing fragment ended and an even heartier burst of clapping greeted the final film, an early copy of a TV kinescope of Black and White's classic routine, Robin O'Hood (the Irish pub *lazzi*).

The lights came up. Del James, the pianist we always paid to play at meetings, struck up "The Cuckoo Song" and the show's first live act began. It was Hal Fawkes "lip-syncing" Barbra Streisand singing "People." He'd covered his Brillo-pad hair with a hideous orange wig and wore a balloon of material meant to be interpreted as a dress. I knew that was the idea because of the immense twin protrusions at top. During the routine, he dropped one, and it turned out to be a cantaloupe.

It wasn't my brand of humor and I would have gone to the john, but I didn't want to miss any of the skit.

The playlet was excellent, funny and meaningful all at once. Jack Black's cameo as Fin/God was delightful, but that wasn't the only merit. The underlying serious theme of the skit was that Adam and Eve were basically simple people innocently duped into eating the apple. Thus the choice of Laurel and Hardy for the Biblical roles.

Wayne Poe was next. A good opportunity to go to the men's room. I excused myself and walked up the aisle, idly scanning the crowd to find Frank Butler. He was nowhere to be seen.

Now I probably have told the details of the next few minutes to the police at least a dozen times, which is understandable since I own a private investigator's license, and they know it. But the fact is I saw very little—a pair of feet behind a stall in the john; Phil Faxon waiting near the back entrance of the kitchen (converted to an entryway) to go on and announce the next act; O. J. by the dais talking to Chuck McCann, but keeping one eye on Poe in hopes he'd do well enough to prove O. J. right in putting him on the show.

But Poe didn't have a chance. Several of the people who couldn't stand him heckled his lousy material, most of which, as Natie'd guessed, had been used the year before. When I emerged from the men's room, a lot of people were talking, paying no attention to Poe, and the laughs were few.

"Now I'd like to tell you about the farmer who shaved his chickens so they'd lay more eggs, but the idea was crazy because they all got sunstroke. Which only goes to prove that a henny shaved is a henny burned."

The audience groaned.

"Or there was the man who hated seagulls and used to throw rocks at them. He left no tern unstoned."

Louder groans.

"And how about the strict schoolteacher who left no stern untoned?"

Hisses.

"Don't forget the lousy Scottish cook who left no scone unburned."

Somebody yelled, "GIVE 'IM THE HOOK!"

"Who was that?" Poe asked, smiling his poisonous grin. "How about standing up?"

Jimmy O'Hara, too dumb to know not to challenge Poe on his own ground, rose to his feet. Jimmy was a loud-mouth kid who just passed the age requirement for joining the Sons. Noisy, but harmless. His friends tried to make him take his seat, but he stood there, grinning.

"Hey, Mr. Poe, your mother ever have any kids?" he called.

"Yeah, kid. I used to have sort of a Siamese Twin, looked just like you. We were separated at an early age: exactly eight days."

It took a fraction of a second for the implication to sink in. There was a general shocked intake of breath, and a little laughter. The kid stood there, vacuous, until a friend whispered in his ear. Then Jimmy blushed beet-red and sat down fast.

"Hey, kid, I'm sorry, I was just kidding," Poe continued, unrelenting, "I know you're sensitive about your upbringing. It's not often they throw out the child and raise the afterbirth."

This time the hiss of indrawn breath sounded like an overstressed steam radiator. Someone booed.

Poe glared. "All right, anybody else want to tackle the master?"

"*I do*." The voice, cutting through the growing sounds of discontent, rang out clearly, unmistakably. It was Hilary. She stood up, hands on hips, waiting for Poe to make the initial assay.

He shaded his eyes and scanned the audience until he spotted her. Sawing his hand in a gesture of dismissal, he said, condescendingly, "Sit down, babe, it won't be a fair fight."

"True, but I'm willing to wait while you run out and buy some brains from a butcher."

A few people tittered.

"Hey, now, look, chick," Poe protested, "I'm tryin' to spare you—"

"Spare us all. Drop dead."

"HAW!" It sounded like Frank Butler. I still didn't know where he was, but the noise came from the direction of the head table.

Poe pointed to Hilary and spoke to the rest of the audience. "You ever see it to fail? Broad can't make it with anybody, she

70

comes on like Godzilla.'' He smiled at her venomously. ''I'll give ya a break, see me in my dressing room.''

''Why not?'' Hilary replied. ''You're probably funnier in bed than onstage.''

That fetched a good guffaw and some applause. Poe's lips pursed tight, but instead of continuing the battle, he turned to Del James and with great emphasis, said ''*Now!*'' Del struck up the lead-in to ''Comedy Tonight'' from *A Funny Thing Happened* . . .

Hilary sat down and Poe started singing. But the audience had tasted blood. First a few catcalls, then a whole chorus of jeers drowned out the music.

Poe ignored the audience, singing as loud as he could, but slowly edged toward the exit to the kitchen, anxious to finish the number and make a fast getaway. Del stepped up the tempo, doing his bit to get Poe the hell out of there. By the final verse—the one with the lyric guaranteeing ''a happy ending, of course''—the singer was almost tiptoe-poised to zoom offstage. He bellowed the final elongated ''Comedy . . . tonight!'' with his arms spread wide in the customary sell-the-end-of-the-song attitude.

At that instant, a great bellow welled from behind the head table. Rising from its concealing drapery, Frank Butler stood erect, hefting with both hands a four-tier, spun-sugar milky-white wedding cake, the tallest, sloppiest such confection I'd ever seen. He leaped onto the platform, his weight shaking the stage; he resembled an angry white pachyderm.

''*Teach you to screw around with the Old Man!*'' Butler roared, mushing the monstrous bonbon into Wayne Poe's face. It happened so quickly that the comic didn't have time to do anything but stand there, astonished, and take the cake.

A tidal wave of rejoicing: snickers, chortles, Woody Woodpecker-type cackling, brouhaha, belly laughs. The tubby avenging angel bowed low to the audience and strutted off.

Poe, inundated with icing, wobbled about with the gigantic cake stuck to his head. Struggling to breathe, he frantically clawed away enough to reveal a snowy suspicion of his features, making everyone howl all the louder.

The comic, apparently determined to make the best of the

71

absurd figure he cut, yammered and flapped his arms like a chicken, sinking to his knees in a limp-legged crumple that would have made Marcel Marceau proud. But he didn't let the gag die there. Allowing the weight of the cake to tilt him, Poe flopped to the floor, his only points of contact his legs and head. With his body angled upwards, he resembled a gigantic half-open jackknife.

The laughter accelerated. The controlled topple was funny enough in itself, but the protracted milking of the ridiculous angle at which his cake-piled head rested was pure inspiration.

"Will you look at that cat?" Al Kilgore exclaimed gleefully.

"That," said Dick Baldwin, standing near the alcove doorway, "is *economy*!" He giggled.

I looked at my watch, clocking the laugh for Poe, figuring he'd never get a reaction like it again. It was exactly ten minutes of eleven. The second hand swept past the numbers. Five seconds.

The comedian was still in the middle of the stage, immobile, a grotesque tangle of floppy limbs and lopsided layer cake.

Ten seconds. Twelve.

Poe didn't move.

O. J. ambled over to the platform, got up on it, walked a few steps, and stared down at the motionless lump. He frowned.

The laughter gradually tapered off.

"*Gene!*" It was Hilary. Her voice was sharp, urgent.

I was already on my way. Hopping onto the stage, I whirled and held out a hand to stop the curiosity seekers from following.

"He might be sick," I said. "Give him air, don't crowd."

O. J., kneeling upstage of Poe, raised his eyes and spoke low. "He's going to need more than air, Gene. Help me carry him out of sight."

I took one look at Poe and shook my head. I knew better than to move a man with a knife stuck in his back.

"Hilary," I yelled, "call Lou Betterman." I didn't want to panic the crowd by directly naming the police.

I felt Poe's pulse. Nothing. I tried his chest. No heartbeat. I rose and asked a question of the audience.

Fortunately, there were three doctors in the house.

I enlisted sergeants-at-arms immediately, appointing each a different door to guard. O. J. hurried downstairs to explain things to any Lambs staff on the premises.

I wanted to avoid a general announcement, but I knew we were going to be there all damned night, so everyone had to be told. I tried to make it as gentle and diplomatic as possible, but predictably, one person went all hysterical and had to be handed over to one of the physicians. The rest of the group buzzed among themselves.

Frank Butler stomped up to the edge of the platform, an anxious look on his broad face.

"Hey, boy!" he bellowed.

"What?"

"This mean we *ain't* gonna see the Laurel and Hardy pitcher?"

SECOND REEL: *35mm sound*.

"Well, here's another nice mess you've gotten me into!"

Puffing out his flabby cheeks, Inspector Lou Betterman, NYPD, glowered at the roomful of nervous, fidgety onlookers and grumbled, half to himself, "A hundred witnesses, for Chrissake, and nobody sees a goddamn thing!" He pulled at the scraggly tuft he thought was a mustache and shook his head as he regarded the technicians on the platform dusting and measuring and photographing. "That," he said, a bit wistfully, "was a lousy thing to do to a beautiful cake."

Betterman was ticked off at being called out at all, let alone in the middle of the night. A Manhattan-based inspector generally concentrates on desk-side administration, but the murder at The Lambs was too ticklish to be left solely to rank and file. For the first half-hour, he was busy just processing celebrities, soothing them and getting them the hell out of there before the news-ghouls descended to scratch up tidbits.

"C'mon," the inspector said, jerking his head for me to follow, "the others are waiting for us in the library." He lumbered across the room, flipping an offhand nod at the officer posted by the rear archway to pass me through.

Inside, the inspector waddled over to a red leather chair and plopped heavily on it. I sat down between Hilary and O. J. while Betterman glared at the fourth person in the room.

Frank Butler, oblivious to the policeman's scrutiny, sat at a small card table engrossed in a hand of Klondike. Every so often, he sneaked peeks at the face-down cards.

"How come," said Betterman to Hilary in a reproachful tone, "you never gimme a call unless it's on business? It'd hurt you to pick up a phone now and then, say hello?"

His acquaintanceship with my employer went back to a time when, according to him, he bounced her on his knee. I found it

77

hard to visualize, not so much because of the difficulty of picturing a tiny Hilary submitting to the familiarity as because of the seeming impossibility of anyone getting past Lou's lap to attain a perch on his patella.

"I don't think," Hilary said quietly, "that you asked us in here for small talk."

"Might as well have," he grumped, "for all I've got. No witnesses. Nobody recognizes the—*will you cut that out*?"

Butler looked up, offended. "All I'm doing's shuffling! What's eatin' you, your truss too tight?"

Betterman waved a warning finger. "You better watch your ass, Butler, or I'll have your license."

The other laughed. "How? I don't operate in this crummy state."

"We can talk to people in Philly."

"Yeah?" Butler snorted, wiping his huge forehead with a disreputable old rag. "They better be pretty hotsy-totsy. My uncle's the chief of police, and the mayor's my second cousin."

Betterman eyed me dubiously. "He on the level?"

"I doubt it."

O. J. cleared his throat, not wanting to interrupt, but having no choice. "Inspector, I—I've got to get back out there. This banquet is my responsibility."

"Yeah. This won't take too long." The policeman withdrew a small notebook and pencil from a pocket, flipped open the pad and made a few notes, then pointed to O. J. with the writing stub. "The way I understand it, you were up by the head table when the incident occurred, right?"

O. J. nodded but did not look directly at Betterman.

"That means you were the only other person in line to see what happened. Did you, in fact, see anybody behind the platform?"

O. J. hesitated before replying. He took out a white handkerchief as if to dab the perspiration from his brow, but forgot what the original intention was, stared at the cloth for a few seconds, then put it back in his pocket. "I . . . I'm afraid I saw no one," he told the policeman at last. "I doubt if anyone noticed anything but the tower of glop Frank here shoved into Poe's face."

"All right," Betterman sighed. "Pass on that for now. Gene

has fixed the time of death—assuming the knife was thrown at the instant the cake—ah—''

Butler wouldn't permit him to find a delicate phrasing. ''Y'mean when I smooshed it in that turkey's fat puss.''

''I'm talking to Mr. Wheete, no one else!'' Betterman said sharply.

''Suits me,'' the Old Man shrugged, repeatedly cutting the deck with one hand.

Betterman closed his eyes for a three-count before continuing.

''All right. Say the stabbing was at—impact, or a second or two later. That was ten of eleven, right?''

O. J.'s normally unclouded brow wrinkled in concentration. ''It sounds correct, sir. I looked at my watch, as a matter of fact, more than once. I was worried Poe might go on too long. Everybody had warned me about that. So you see, I was really more concerned with the passage of time than the exact hour.''

Hilary raised an index finger. Betterman nodded for her to speak.

''Lou, you said the knife was *thrown*?''

''Looks it. We figure the killer hadda be back by the kitchen door, eight or nine feet behind Poe to hit at the angle we found the knife. Couldn't've been too close behind. Poe was on a platform and the angle woulda been too low.''

''Any chance,'' Hilary asked, ''the blow could have been delivered by a person standing in the wings behind him, *on* the platform?''

The inspector jerked a thumb at Butler and O. J. ''These two'd have t'be practically blind to miss seeing anybody standing there. The kitchen door, all right, that I can buy. It's on a lower level and in the shadows.''

He looked at O. J. and the Old Man, hoping one of them would remember something, but O. J. just studied his manicure and Butler began building a card castle.

I understood Butler's callousness. He, like most of the Sons, hated Wayne Poe. But he was really nettling Lou Betterman.

''It's a good thing for you,'' the policeman told him, ''that you were on the other side of the victim when you delivered that cake. Otherwise, you'd be my prime suspect.''

79

"Crap, boy! That creep wasn't worth the trouble to kill, I just wanted to make him look like a horse's ass." Butler's house of cards tumbled to the table and he scowled at them. "Need a shot of gin. Hands ain't steady enough."

"Lou," I said, "have you questioned Phil Faxon yet? I recall he was standing at the back of the room near the alcove where you go into the kitchen. Maybe he saw the killer leaving through the kitchen door near the stairs."

The inspector hailed the nearby patrolman and asked him to pass the word along to Katz, Betterman's assistant, to find Phil Faxon.

While we were waiting, Hilary asked about the murder weapon.

"Smudged beyond recognition. No prints," said the inspector.

"You mean somebody wiped it off?"

"Nobody got near the body," I interrupted.

"Chrissake, it hadda be cleaned beforehand," said Betterman, waving a paw at me impatiently. "Killer probably wore gloves, though so far that's conjecture."

"Where did the knife come from?" asked Hilary. "The kitchen?"

"Nope. You never saw a dagger like this in a chef's mitt. It's honed razor-sharp, perfectly balanced, single ruby in the side of the hilt—"

"There are a number of trophies all over the club, hanging up, in display cases," said O. J. "It's probably one of them."

Betterman frowned. "If it is, nobody recognizes it. Your vice-president, what's-his-name?"

"Hal Fawkes."

"He says he never saw a knife like that in the club. I checked with one of the Lambs officials downstairs, and he confirms."

Hilary had a puzzled look on her face. "Lou," she said, "can I get a look at it before you tag it and pack it away?"

"Ask Katz when he gets back with Faxon. Why, you know something?"

She shook her head. "Not anything I can brag about. Just a niggling feeling, that's all, I can't define it."

Katz, a sad-eyed policeman, cleared his throat and passed Hal Fawkes into the room. Betterman barked at Katz before he could back out.

"I said Faxon, not Fawkes."

Katz nodded long-sufferingly. He was used to his superior's irascibility. "Faxon's upstairs with the old guy, waitin' for the ambulance to—"

"*Hah*?" Betterman rose with the grace of a hippo. "What old guy? Who's sick?"

"Jackie Black," said Hal, scratching his Brillo-pad hair. As usual, he provided no information beyond the bare facts.

"Who the hell's Jack Black? What *is* this stuff about an ambulance?" Betterman demanded, looking from Hal to the detective.

Katz spoke. "Jack Black, the old man. He's not feeling well."

O. J. rose, his brow contracting in worry. "Officer, Mr. Black is past ninety. We brought him from a rest home, and he should have been on his way back to bed by now."

Betterman stared sourly at Katz. "Did you call for an ambulance, or are you waiting for me to burp you?"

"It's on the way, Lou."

"Good. Pack the old futz in, then I wanna see Faxon down here."

Katz started to go, but Hilary hailed him. The inspector, remembering his suggestion, told the detective to let her look at the murder weapon when he was finished.

"I think," said Hal, rubbing absently at the stubble now adorning his cheeks, "we better call a special board meeting tomorrow, O. J."

"Why?" O. J. asked.

"I don't know," Hal replied with equal innocence. "Just figured we should."

O. J. shook his head. "The soonest I can convene the committee is Wednesday."

"How come so late?" I asked.

"The by-laws," O. J. answered.

I had to think a moment to realize what he meant.

81

When last-minute emergency committee meetings have to be called to bail the president out of the clink, or for a similar foreseeable likelihood, the president shall use his one phone call to get the vice-president to notify the rest of the committee. Three days notice shall be given . . .

It was already Sunday morning, so a committee session technically could not be convened until Wednesday night.

It was the first time I'd ever heard O. J. worrying about sticking to the letter of the by-law.

Nothing new was added by Faxon, or anyone else, including me. I was so sleepy I could hardly keep my eyes open during the questioning and certain points I meant to bring up slipped my mind because of fatigue. As for Faxon, he'd been riveting his attention on the stage during the Poe-Butler collision, so if anyone did leave by way of the kitchen, he missed seeing them.

It was nearly dawn when Hilary said we could leave. She was worn out, too, and despite my trepidation, allowed Frank Butler to pick up his Packard and drive us home. She insisted he sack out in our apartment. It was much too early to unleash him on the roads of New Jersey and Pennsylvania.

He drove fairly carefully, for him, only wobbling once or twice into the wrong lane. At 70th Street, he stopped and double-parked long enough to dash into an all-night Pick & Pay. He emerged a moment later with a bag loaded high with Colt 45 cans and several bags of walnuts.

We must have looked pretty bedraggled to the doorman. He politely averted his eyes as Hilary and I entered and probably wondered what we'd been doing all evening. Whatever he thought, it must have been more fun than what we'd been through. I told him to let Butler in after he parked the car.

As Hilary closed the door and switched on the dimmest office light, I asked her where Butler should be bedded down for the night (or, more accurately, morning).

"Let him sleep in your bed."

I yawned. "And I get the couch?"

"Don't be dense," Hilary smiled. "I don't take up *that* much room, you know . . ."

I set the bag of beer and nuts on the desk and walked over to

83

Hilary. She rested her head against my chest and we stood there a moment in weary, but not unpleasant proximity.

"Don't get any ideas, brightness," she murmured, "I'm totally exhausted."

"Me, too."

There was a pounding at the door. We ignored it for one gentle second, then moved away from one another and I let the Old Man in.

He stumped to the couch, sat down, and sighed deeply. "Been a long night, even for me, boy. Hand me some medicine."

I fished out a can of Colt 45. He ripped off the tab and took a long swallow. Hilary suggested a glass but he shook his head. "Takes too long, sis. Like Heywood Broun says, 'Make hay when you've got moonshine!' "

Hilary blinked, groggy with the simple logic of Butler's misappropriated philosophy. She turned to me. "Gene," she asked, "do you think this clown could possibly have had anything to do with Poe's death?"

I shook my head. "Not his style. Cake bashing's more his thing. Right, Old Man?"

He nodded and sipped, a look of pure contentment on his face. "I couldn't've stabbed the bastard, I had both hands full. What a hell of a gesture!" He finished the malt liquor in a single pull and motioned Hilary to toss him another can. "Got a nutcracker, toots?"

"Yes. You're not going to start with them *now*?"

His eyebrows shot up. "I'm hungry."

"Look," I told her, "go to bed, I'll fix him a sandwich or something and bed him down in the 'guest room.' "

"I don't need no sandwich, just a nutcracker."

"I'm getting it, I'm getting it," Hilary replied, resigned. She knew we must have one somewhere, but which drawer was anyone's guess.

While she was out of the room, Butler talked about the upcoming Philadelphia/New York convention. I was too bushed to stem the tide, but finally I pointed out that the whole thing might have to be canceled because of the fiasco of the past evening.

"Why? What's one got to do with another?"

"I don't know, but O. J. is calling an emergency meeting of the executive committee to discuss it."

"When? I better be there."

"Wednesday night, probably. O. J. hasn't said."

"Wednesday?" Hilary repeated, entering with the nutcracker, which she handed to him. "Maybe I should come along, I might be able to help. I've got a few—"

"Sons committee meetings," I said quickly, "are closed to nonmembers, Hilary."

"No problem." She walked to her desk. "I'll write a check for membership dues. How much—and to whom do I give it?"

I was stuck. I didn't know whether to blurt out the truth or let the folly proceed unchecked. Butler decided it for me.

Cracking open a walnut and picking at the meat with his stubby fingers, he informed her that she could not join the Sons of the Desert.

Her back stiffened.

"Why not?"

"You can join the Philly tent, toots, but not the parent chapter in this burg." He cracked another walnut.

"Why not?" she repeated, not loud. She was standing poker-stiff, staring at me, daring me to avert my eyes.

"You can't," said Butler, "because you're a broad."

A long silence.

"Is he telling the truth?" she asked me.

My mouth was so dry I had to swallow twice before I could manage to speak.

"It *is* stag," I admitted.

Hilary stared at me with a positively indescribable expression. It made me feel terrible without knowing exactly why. If she'd only sworn or uttered something sarcastic or demanded a reason why I hadn't told her sooner, I could have coped. But she just looked at me, and I had to turn away.

After a long moment, she left the room.

Hilary closed her bedroom door behind her. Very gently.

But I slept on the couch.

Butler was gone by the time I woke, and so was Hilary. No note. I had nothing to do because it was Sunday, so after a while I left the apartment and strolled along Broadway, stopping for lunch at the Maravilla, an inexpensive Chinese-Cuban restaurant between 84th and 85th.

I put away some soup, a banana omelette, and a glass of house wine, then returned to West End Avenue, but still no Hilary. I moped around for a while, did the *Times* acrostic, went out again and browsed for half an hour at the Barqu, purchasing a couple of secondhand paperbacks, then headed home again.

Four-thirty. The place still was empty. It was too nice a day to spend indoors, especially in an apartment cloaked by the hush of a New York summer Sunday. More strolling. Riverside Drive. Children tossing Frisbees. Optimists at water's edge beneath the trestle trying to fish the Hudson. Daylight lasted late, and there was still an angry crimson streaking to the clouds hanging over New Jersey as I headed back to Broadway along 93rd. I toyed with the notion of catching a double feature James Bond at the Symphony, changed my mind and took a light supper, ginger trout and cider, at the Sou-En.

It was nearly nine o'clock when I opened the door, sure Hilary would be home in time to catch the latest goings-on at 165 Eaton Place. But I was wrong. I watched Mrs. Bridges fix dinner for the king by myself, distracted partially by Jean Marsh's offbeat, chilly sensuality, but mostly preoccupied with unanswered questions as to Hilary's whereabouts.

She didn't reappear in the apartment till Monday morning. I was opening the mail when she walked in, asked if there were any messages, then went back to change for a press luncheon at the Sign of the Dove.

She refused to answer any questions I had unless they had to do with business. For all the mind she paid me, I might still have been alone.

The deep-freeze lasted until Wednesday evening, the night O. J. called the emergency session of the Sons board.

Wednesday. 7:30 P.M.

I was going out the door when I saw Hilary pulling on her coat.

"I'm going with you, Gene."

"You can't!"

Her blue eyes fixed me icily. "Are you going to stop me?"

Her hair, tied in a severe backknot, was a sure sign I was in disfavor.

We shared a taxi in silence.

7:50 P.M.

Seated at the big round table in The Lambs were O. J., Hal, Natie, Phil, and Toby. They were all busy stuffing folded papers into envelopes bearing the Sons of the Desert escutcheon.

At the end of the table, Frank Butler sat idly puffing on a twisted cigar like a fat, malignant dragon.

O. J. greeted Hilary pleasantly and suggested she wait in the adjacent restaurant. "The meeting won't be too long, I'll try to get Gene back to—"

"I'm staying," she said, plopping her purse on the table.

Natie paused with an envelope flap against his tongue tip. Silence. Five sets of eyebrows arched as if controlled by a single muscle. Only the Old Man did not look surprised.

"I want to speak to the committee," said Hilary.

"Go ahead," said Hal, "we haven't started the meeting yet."

"No." She shook her head and sat down next to Natie. "I'm not in the mood just yet."

Five pairs of eyes swung in my direction. Their attitudes ranged from simple disbelief to downright hostility. Butler looked at me with a mixture of amusement and pity.

"Didn't you explain?" Natie asked me.

"I did. You see the result."

"Look, lady," Phil argued, "this is members only here."

Hilary nodded, fishing in her purse. She took out her checkbook and poised her pen to write. "Who here is the treasurer?"

"I am," Natie said, "but I can't take your money."

"There are rules governing choice of members," O. J. tried to explain soothingly, but Hilary cut him off.

"Don't be mealy-mouthed. You mean, it's 'men only.' Right?"

O. J. smiled wanly but said nothing. It was no secret that he wanted to open the club to women members, but was afraid of the opposition.

"Look, lady," Phil said angrily, "this is a private organization meeting in a private club. We can get The Lambs to throw you out."

"I'd like to see anyone try," she replied, smiling frostily.

"Well, goddamnit, I'll toss you out on your ass myself!"

"Phil, sit down!" I ordered him." She's got a black belt in karate."

He sat.

Frank Butler chuckled. "Well, boys," he said, "this situation is no skin off my tongue—we're integrated at the Two Tars—but let me tell you, this broad is tougher than a crocogator. Take my advice and don't hassle her."

There was a lot more grumbling, and no one was too pleased with me, but Hilary stayed.

8:05 P.M.

We all stood, including Hilary, while O. J. said a few words of tribute to Jack Black, who'd died in the hospital shortly after the banquet.

As we sat, Hal murmured glumly that he didn't know how to break the news to his uncle.

"Billy doesn't know?" O. J. asked.

Hal shook his head. "I've been putting it off. Second death in less than a month, and the first one brought on the stroke. I'm scared to give the old guy another jolt."

O. J. patted Hal on the shoulder. "If it's not too late, maybe we can call him after the meeting—sort of ease him into it. Then we can take a run up there Saturday and break it to him."

Phil laughed. "Gonna tell 'im his partner's on the roof, huh? Y'know that joke?"

We all knew it, and none of us laughed.

8:07 P.M.

"Gimme one-a them," a loud voice demanded. I turned and saw Dutchy, late as usual, trying to hold himself steadily. His eyes were out of focus and he swayed a little.

O. J. helped him sit down. Dutchy flapped absently at one protruding ear and squinted at the flyer in an unsuccessful attempt to bring it into sync with his fogged vision.

Suddenly he looked up. "Who the hell's that?" He meant Hilary.

O. J. did his best to explain; having no explanation, it wasn't easy. Dutchy frowned, then promptly forgot about her. He waved the flyer. "What the hell's this?"

"Emergency flyers," Natie called across the table. "Apologizing for the mess at the banquet."

"And it's also got the pertinent poop about our double blast," Butler said.

"Speaking of which," said Natie gleefully, "a lot of checks have already come in. We're gonna have a crowd of Sons going to Philly."

"Which brings up the question," Hal observed, "of whether or not we are going to charter a bus."

Natie groaned.

Eventually it got put to a vote, though technically I don't think we had a quorum. But it was only because there were so few people present that we could so easily dispose of the bus issue—by the simple expedient of dumping the whole responsibility in O. J.'s lap.

8:45 P.M.

"If there is no further business," O. J. began, but he didn't finish his sentence. Hilary stood up and stared from one to the other of us with great displeasure.

"I don't believe you people!"

O. J. looked at her blankly. "What's the matter?"

"In spite of your adolescent membership policy," she replied, "there is a deal of good in the Sons, I must admit. I enjoyed the banquet. So I came here to help, even though I despise your chauvinistic exclusion of women. But—"

"What's she talkin' about?" Dutchy grumbled, vainly trying to follow the proceedings.

"Yeah, lady, what the hell *are* you talking about?" Phil asked, his face a mass of downturned wrinkles. "Who asked for your help, and what'd we do with it if we had it?"

"I assumed," she said, "you would need suggestions concerning the murder of Wayne Poe. I've been waiting for the question to be brought up, but hardly a word has been mentioned about Saturday night."

"We're sending out the flyers," Hal said, palms up in an attitude of perplexity. "What else should we do?"

"I imagined—it appears wrongly—that you would worry about the scandal and suspicion the killing would bring upon the entire organization (and perhaps certain members in particular). Surely you have all been harassed by the police by now."

Which showed Hilary didn't understand how to hold the attention at a Sons committee meeting. Her comment touched off a rash of simultaneous personal grievances concerning the police. They all spoke at once, and it was impossible for Hilary to keep the floor. She finally sat down, disgusted.

O. J. brought everyone in line. "That's enough communal griping," he said severely, turning to address Hilary. "I don't see what you expected us to do. The murder of Wayne Poe is the police's responsibility, not ours."

"But has it occurred to you," she countered, "that your members may not like harboring a murderer?"

"What's that mean?" Phil growled. "You accusing somebody here—?"

"I'm only suggesting what others might think. For all *I* know, a Lambs waiter hid in the kitchen and threw a knife because of some ancient grudge."

"This whole discussion is irrelevant," O. J. stated. "It's time to adjourn."

"No, hold on, O. J.," said Natie. "Maybe she's right. We don't know what'll happen if the police don't catch the killer. It might hurt membership."

"Well, what do you propose we do about it?"

Natie shrugged. "I dunno. Hire Nero Wolfe?"

"We could conduct a private inquiry," Toby suggested, speaking up for the first time that night.

"You're out of order," O. J. told him.

"Why?"

"Because we can't go prying into the affairs of our members. We have no official status to do so and it would make us very unpopular."

"So hire a detective, it's not such a bad idea after all," Phil said.

"We can't afford one," Natie objected.

Hilary looked at me, waiting for me to suggest her for the job, but I kept my mouth shut. We were already in enough financial difficulty at the office without dissipating more client time by sleuthing, for which we never seemed to earn a penny.

"Hey, you dummies," Butler rasped, lighting a stogie from the butt of the previous one, "don't you know I'm a detective? Gimme expenses in gas and stuff, I'll catch this character and give 'im a goddamn medal!"

Most of the committee thought the proposal a good one, and all spoke again at once, thanking Butler for the offer. But when the talk died down, O. J. protested.

"Investigating our members is not a proper pursuit of this committee! And furthermore, Frank is a Pennsylvania operative. He has no license for this state."

"So?" the Old Man shrugged. "Gene here has a New York license. Right, boy?"

"How do you know that? Did *I* tell you?"

"Saw it on your wall that time I was over. How's about it, boy, you and me can work together, huh?"

I glanced fearfully at Hilary. She sat erect, looking pale, but said nothing.

"I don't think," I murmured, "that I'd better do that."

9:08 *P.M.*

O. J. had Hilary at the bar, buying her a drink and talking earnestly to her, presumably asking her to mind her own business, not the Sons'.

Natie approached me. "Gene, you'd better think about things a little better next time."

"What do you mean?"

"I mean, bringing women to closed committee meetings."

"I didn't bring her. She came by herself."

"You came in together." Phil waggled a finger at me. "You try this again, we'll blackball you outta the Sons."

"Phil, we don't have a blackballing procedure," Natie said.

"We don't? How 'bout when we threw out Brad Chelsea?"

"Naah, naah," Dutchy joined in, leaning on Phil's shoulder for support, "we blabbed for four hours about how to get rid of 'im, but the only reason he stopped coming is he moved out of the city. We could never figure how to throw out one member and not set a precedent." He turned to me. "How come we're talking about blackballing?"

"Phil says I should be blackballed for bringing Hilary."

"See?" Phil crowed. "You admit you brought her!"

"No, I didn't, dammit! I didn't want Hilary to come, but she's so pigheaded stubborn—"

I stopped.

Across the room, Hilary was listening to every word.

93

9:12 P.M.

It was a short argument, but bitter. Hilary walked out by herself. O. J. bought me a boilermaker and I gloomily downed it while Frank Butler sat by me, keeping pace, swig for swig.

"If you're pissed off at Hilary," he said, "show her you can do what you damn well please."

"Meaning what?"

"Meaning I saw how she looked when they wanted you and me to team up. She stared daggers."

"That she did."

"So if that idea bugs her, then c'mon, give the Old Man a hand, and I'll show you how to be a *real* detective!" He puffed out his chest like a child of my generation playing Mussolini.

"Sure, sure," I kidded, "why not? Call me Watson from now on."

But Butler didn't understand irony. He immediately told O. J. and the others that I'd decided to help him investigate Poe's murder. O. J. launched into a tirade against the plan, and the rest of the committee wrangled with the president.

I gave up and headed for the door. Butler chugged behind me.

"I'll give ya a lift, boy, and we can discuss strategy."

My head was aching as usual after a committee meeting, and I was in too much discomfort to argue with the Old Man. I even let him pile me into his decrepit Packard because I wanted to get home and talk to Hilary.

9:23 P.M.

In the car, I asked him where on earth he'd ever come up with a portmanteau word like crocogator.

"Aw, ain't you never hearda one? The crocogator's the meanest critter in the world. Got the head of a alligator on one end and the head of a crocodile on the other."

"Which means he can't—"

"Kee-rect, boy," he interrupted. "That's what makes 'im so fierce . . ."

94

Butler double-parked in front of the building and came in to use the bathroom.

Hilary wasn't home. I found a note from her on my typewriter.

Gene, we've quarreled before, but this is entirely different. My father used his connections to prevent me from securing a state detective license. Yet I tried to win his approval. What did I get out of it? He doesn't even like to admit I'm his daughter.
Tonight reminded me of that situation. The Sons is important to you, so I made an effort—like a damn fool. I've been worried about money lately. Maybe it makes sense for us to end our business and personal relationships at the same time. What do you think?
Hilary

Also on my desk was a phone message in Hilary's handwriting, a note to call Penny Saxon.

Salt on the wound.

"What's the matter, boy?" Butler asked, wiping his water-moist hands on his vest. "You look like you've been sucking a sump pump."

I handed him the letter.

"Oh, hell, I'm sorry, boy," he said after he'd finished reading. "Y'know what Shakespeare says, though—hell hath no fury like a woman!"

Couldn't he ever attribute a quote correctly?

Dear Hilary,

Maybe we'd better stay out of each other's hair a few days till we cool off and think things over. Frank Butler has invited me to spend some time in Philly, and I've accepted. If you want me for any reason, the phone number is on my Wheeldex.

I put the note on her bed so she'd spot it first thing. Then, hefting my suitcase, I told the Old Man I was ready to leave. He put down the bottle, wiped his lips, and started for the front door.

The phone rang.

After six, I say "Ms. Quayle's residence," but the caller wanted me. I identified myself, wondering where I'd heard the grating voice before.

"I hear," he said, "that you and that old futz think you can catch me . . ."

"Who is this?"

Silence.

"*Who is this?*"

A low, unctuous chuckle.

"Who I am is none of your friggin' business, buster. But stay out of this, or you might wind up like Poe, you and that fat clown."

He hung up.

I told Butler what I'd heard.

"That son-of-a-bitch!" he howled. "Think he can scare the Old Man?" Butler yanked out his rusty .45, and waved it wildly in the air. "I'll blow so many holes in the bastard he'll look like a puzzle without all the pieces!"

"Put the gun away, for God's sake! Don't you know better than to point that thing?"

He stuck it back in its holster. "You say you recognized the voice, boy? Who the hell was it?"

"I only said it sounded like someone I'd heard before."

"Who?"

"Wayne Poe."

Thursday, June 21

By the time I woke up on Butler's lumpy couch, he was already back in the office working on a case. Of Colt 45.

"Morning," I grunted. "She call?"

"Nope." He gestured in the direction of the refrigerator. "Help yourself to some breakfast."

I opened it. There was nothing inside but beer.

At half past one, Butler folded his issue of the *National Enquirer*, rose and locked the office door, though I couldn't imagine why, since no one had come in all morning.

He lifted a small rabbit-eared TV set from behind a file cabinet, set it on his desk, and switched it on to NBC.

"You watch 'Days of Our Lives'?" I asked, astonished.

"Yep."

"*Why?*"

"Because it's got the best goddamn broads on the tube!" he said, stretching his feet onto a dilapidated hassock and clasping his hands over his ample belly. He sighed contentedly.

I started to ask him how long he'd been hooked, but he waved me down impatiently. "Shaddap, Amanda's sick!"

It was obvious he was as caught up in the plot as any housewife. I didn't have anything else to do, so I sat down and watched with him, wondering who the hell everyone was and how they were related. He tried to fill me in during the commercials, but the complications made me giddy.

I had to admit he was right, though, about the women. They were stunningly lovely. One of them gave me a jolt when she appeared on the screen.

She looked almost exactly like Hilary.

98

Butler spent the previous evening at a Two Tars board meeting and I took a ride over to visit my old friend, Marty Gold, whom I knew in New York, but who now worked at the Einstein medical facilities in northern Philly.

Friday morning some work came in for the Old Man. His business, such as it was, consisted mainly of trailing erring spouses and getting their indiscretions on Polaroid.

"I always make two pix of each exposure," he explained. "One for the client, one for the files." He winked at me broadly.

I warned him about the possible consequences of blackmail, but he vigorously shook his head.

"I just like t'look at the pitchers."

The phone rang. I almost reached for it, then remembered it wasn't my office. Butler took it. As soon as he heard the voice on the other end, his face converted into one immense frown.

"Yeah, I'm busy," he complained, and had to repeat the same phrase in a variety of variant wordings for the next ten minutes. At length, he hung up, shaking his head.

"Who was that?"

"My old lady."

"Your wife?"

He shook his head. "My maw."

Butler tramped over to the refrigerator, opened the door, and took out a Colt 45. Popping the tab, he took a long swig and then gestured around the room with the can. "This whole place is her money," he said glumly. "Never lets me forget it." He stared distastefully at the malt beverage. "That's why I can't drink during working hours. She won't let me."

"But you're drinking, Old Man."

"You call this drinking? This just keeps my tonsils from drying up." He shook his head. "Like the guy says, 'Booze does more than Milton Berle,' only the old lady don't believe it!"

"She doesn't have to know, does she?"

He sat, looking tired. "She sends the damn clan to spy on me. 'Good old Uncle Frank,' like I was some damn clown! Cripes,

what a tribe! If they see any hard stuff around while I'm
workin', the old lady storms in, pours out all my special-blend
gin—''

"Special-blend *gin*?''

"—and fills the bottles with water, which she makes me
drink! Gaah!'' He spit out the end of a twist cigar and set a
match to the other end. Butler puffed on it, a sour look on his
face.

I cheered him up when I pointed out it was time to tune in on
Julie and Doug.

Saturday, June 23

Still no call. I was sure I'd hear from her by the weekend.

Butler was busy till noon with a succession of seedy, shady-
looking clients, so I took a long walk on Chestnut, Broad, and
Walnut streets trying to sort out my feelings.

A little after twelve, I returned and offered to take him to
lunch.

"Swell,'' he said, "but I'm paying. You're unemployed.''

"That's not official yet.''

Butler bit his lip and worried it for several seconds before
replying. "Uh-h-h . . . I hate t'tell you, boy, but—''

"But what?'' I felt suddenly chilly.

"I called your office yesterday. Thought I'd smooth things
out for ya.''

"And? What did Hilary say?''

"Didn't talk t'her. A man answered.''

I digested the barbed bit of information. "Did he sound like
he was just visiting?''

"Nope. Gave me the formal secretary business, boy, said she
was out and could he take any messages.''

It set my head spinning, the celerity with which I'd been
replaced. I reached for the phone, determined to find out who
Hilary had hired, but just then the Old Man emitted a dismayed
yell. I turned and saw him standing by the door to the stairwell.

"Cripes! It's the clan!'' He ran to his desk, grabbed a false
nose and goatee from a drawer, and plastered them on his face.

100

"Lock the door—it's my sister's monsters! They'll expect me to take the whole carload out to eat!"

He ran to a closet, found a strange-looking hat, and jammed it on his head, then made me follow him down the back stairs.

We emerged into a dark alley even narrower than Camac Street. He started one way loping like a hippopotamus in panic, then changed his mind and turned, almost knocking me down.

"They're too damn smart, they'll try to head us off that way," he said. "Go the other direction!"

Just then, there was a chorus of young voices from the end of the alley he'd just turned away from. "Uncle Frank! Uncle Frank!"

"RUN!" he roared. Though I'm in better shape than Butler, he left me far behind, clearing the other end of the long corridor by a good quarter-block before I emerged into the side street.

Butler was way across the street yanking open the door of the Packard. He climbed in, started it with a lurch, zoomed over to the curb, and frantically gesticulated for me to get in. I did, slamming the door hard.

If he'd been on the Le Mans track he yearned for at that moment, he might have established a world record. Next thing I knew, when the scenery stopped blurring, we were on South Street, blocks away from his family.

When I could catch my breath, I asked whether he wasn't afraid they'd blab to his mother how he'd run out on them.

"You forget, boy," he chuckled, a sly look on his face, "I'm in disguise. They can't prove it was me!"

He honestly believed he'd fooled them.

It was his treat. He took me to Levis', a hot dog emporium that deserves all the reputation that Nathan's lays claim to.

It was a dingy place, with old wooden chairs and formica-top tables, but the hot dogs were 100 percent beef, the mustard was tangy, and the soda fountain was the original one that had been in operation on the day the store opened back in the latter years of the nineteenth century. Levis' had a reputation for being open twenty-four hours every day of the year, including holidays. On the wall were huge rosters of names of fifty-year customers of the frankfurter mecca; some of them were from Main Line and Bala Cynwyd social registers.

An elegantly clad young woman stood at the hot dog counter. She fished out some change from a purse and as she did, a dime fell into the immense relish bowl. A big plastic paddle that looked like an oversize doctor's tongue depressor was in the bowl. She took it and daintily tried to work the coin out, but every time it neared the top edge, it slid back into the condiment.

"Could you help me?" she begged the fat attendant behind the counter, a woman with frizzled hair and a gold tooth in place of one of her incisors.

"Sho', honey," she grinned, plunging her sweaty hand into the relish. She brought the dime out surrounded by pickle, and her customer took the coin with a shudder.

I bought two franks, a chocolate soda, and a plate of pickled tomatoes and joined Butler, who munched on a fish cake.

"Now what're we gonna do," he asked, "about finding that bird who stabbed Poe and threatened us?"

"I don't know. Can't say I really care, either."

"*I* say we rough 'em all up, till one of them tells us what we want to know!"

"You can't do that, Old Man."

"Why not?"

I didn't bother to lecture him on the dim view the police take concerning assault and battery. I merely pointed out that if he wanted to get some answers, he had to question at least six people.

"It can't be anybody else," I explained. "It's either Natie, Toby, O. J., Hal, Phil, or Dutchy."

"How come?"

"Because they're the only ones besides you, me, and Hilary who heard we might be investigating Poe's death. Of that group, now I think of it, you can eliminate Toby, too."

"Why?"

"He wasn't feeling well, and left right after the skit that night. He wasn't there when Poe got killed."

"Any candidates among the others?" Butler asked. I was amused. For the past two days, he'd taken every opportunity to instruct me on the art of detecting, ignoring the fact I already had my own license. But when it came right down to the brainwork, he wanted my opinion.

I told him about Dutchy sneaking upstairs when he supposedly was not yet in the club.

"Think he could've made his voice sound like Poe's?"

"That's what bothers me, Old Man. There's only one good candidate for that."

He nodded. "I been thinking about Phil Faxon, too."

"Uh-huh. And he's got a motive—admittedly an ancient one." I told Butler about the time Poe got Faxon in trouble with organized crime.

"Okay," he said, wiping his lips with a paper napkin, "so I'll beat Phil's ass around the room till he spills what he knows."

I shook my head. "There's two things wrong with him as a candidate."

"Yeah?"

"First off, why would he wait fifteen years to get even? Second, why would he telephone and imitate Poe's voice?"

"So's we wouldn't know who he was!"

"Uh-uh. Everybody knows Phil is a crackerjack vocal mimic. It's just too obvious."

Butler blinked, beyond his depth.

We talked some more about it, but I didn't give a damn who killed Wayne Poe, and I told Butler as far as I was concerned, the case was his and his alone.

"But I don't have a New York license," he complained.

Which was the Empire State's gain, but I kept my opinion to myself.

Sunday, June 24

I telephoned Hilary.

A man whose voice sounded very familiar answered and told me Hilary was busy.

I stiffened. "Harry, is that *you*?"

"Gene?"

103

"What the hell are you doing answering the phone for her?"

"Looks like there's a new light in the lady's life, wouldn't you say?" He gave it a lilt, but then he would, being an actor.

"She hired you?"

"Bingo, brightness." Her favorite derogatory term sounded quite unpleasant coming from him.

"I want to speak to her."

"You can't. She's questioning somebody."

"Questioning someone? Who? What for?"

"I don't know. Some film expert. Look, I've got to get off. Come on around some time, would you? I need room for my things in the closet."

He hung up.

I couldn't believe she'd make the transfer that fast. A new secretary, all right, but *living space* for Harry, too? But then, why else would he be answering the phone on a Sunday?

Frank Butler walked in. "Hey, boy, glad you're up. Let's strap on the feed bag."

"Old Man " I said deliberately, "can you come up to New York for a couple of days with me?"

His eyes widened, then gleamed with interest. "You bet your butt I can! What's up?"

"You and I have got a murder to investigate."

I wanted to get started early Monday, but we didn't begin the drive to New York till nearly three P.M.

First, Butler had to arrange for his brother to come in and take care of the office. This was a complicated chore.

"See, Andy don't stay still long enough to catch 'im at any one phone " Butler explained. "I gotta keep callin' till I luck him in." He pointed to a long list of telephone numbers. "He's liable t'be at any one of these."

The calling went on through Sunday and into Monday morning. He finally located him at 11:30, and his brother showed up in the office at a quarter after one, but by then it was too near "Days of Our Lives" time, so we didn't actually pile into the Packard till mid-afternoon.

Butler sipped Colt 45 and handled the wheel easily and carefully. He was definitely a safer driver when slightly sloshed. I stared moodily at the road ahead and thought about my nemesis, Harry Whelan. I thought that after their mutual trip to Washington (during which Hilary solved the mystery of the Third Murderer in *Macbeth*), she'd dropped the actor from her roster of romantic candidates. What the hell was he doing back in her life?

I also wondered who the "film expert" was she'd been talking to. Surely whatever they'd been discussing related in some way to the Sons of the Desert—how, I had no idea. I wondered, too, if the "expert" was someone on my list of suspects. . . .

What with five o'clock traffic and the late start we got, we didn't emerge from the Lincoln Tunnel till nearly six. I suggested a small hotel, The Seymour, on West 45th. They put the car away for us, and we sat down to rest for a few minutes before deciding what to do next.

I rang up O. J. at home to tell him I was back in town, and to ask if I needed to know anything regarding board meetings or the rapidly approaching Philadelphia New York get-together.

"Everything is fine," he said. "Jerry Freundlich and I just spoke to each other and he says the Two Tars have it all under control. Natie's gotten us a good deal on chartering a bus, one is all we'll need. I hope you and Frank Butler have dropped the crazy idea about prying into the business of Sons members."

"I'm afraid we haven't. In fact—"

"You know I'm very much against this, Gene."

"I know, but we feel we *have* to start asking a few people some questions. Board members, to begin with."

There was a long silence.

"O. J., you still there?"

"Well," he said at last, "I've made *my* wishes clear. I wash my hands of any responsibility."

He hung up before I could say anything else.

The next order of business was to toss a coin and see who would concentrate on whom. Butler drew Phil Faxon, and I got Dutchy. We called both, but no one answered at either number.

The rest of Monday we did nothing more constructive than eat at the Ceylon India and kill a few dollars in a pinball emporium where Butler trimmed me of the cost of a six-pack of Colt 45.

When we got back to the hotel, the contents of the Packard were resting on a table: half a dozen bottles of gin, a large bag of walnuts, and two boxes of twists. Butler took some of each, plopped onto one of the beds, and told me to tune in the wrestling matches.

I did, then tried Phil's number again. No answer. I left a message with his answering device to tell him where we were so he could get in touch. Next I tried Dutchy's house. His wife answered. She told me he wasn't in. Very abruptly. I left a message with her, too.

106

That ended my sleuthing efforts for the day. I asked Butler to hold down the noise and, if possible, to stop hurling walnut shells at the screen whenever he got mad at the referee. Then I took a shower, thought briefly about calling Hilary, rejected the notion, and went to bed.

When I rose Tuesday morning, Butler was snoring like a buzz saw. I washed and got dressed. Then I noticed a corner of white protruding beneath the door.

There was no writing on the outside of the envelope. Inside, a single sheet of cheap scratch paper from a note pad bore a typed message. It was difficult to read. The ribbon should have been changed months earlier.

THIS IS YOUR LAST WARNING.
STAY OUT OF IT. OR SOMEBODY
MAY GET HURT.

I roused Butler and stuck it under his nose. He hopped out of bed and starting pulling on his clothes, swearing all during the process.

I asked the desk clerk whether anyone had inquired about our room number during the night. He said we'd have to ask Mr. Arteseros, who returned to duty at 6 P.M.

After brunch, Butler and I decided to split up, tackle our respective quarries, and meet later in the afternoon. I went to a phone booth and called the Hovis number again. Dutchy was not in. I asked Isabel if she'd mind if I stopped over for a few minutes to ask her something. She wanted to know why I couldn't do it on the phone. I couldn't very well tell her I wanted to watch her face while she was answering, so I made up some lame excuse and she finally gave me a half-hearted invitation to hurry over because she could spare only a few minutes.

The Hovis apartment was in a brownstone on West 26th. A steep set of street-level stairs and four inner flights left me winded. I staggered through the door she opened and dropped onto the nearest chair in the hallway.

"Don't get too comfortable," she warned me, "I'm about to go out." She was adjusting a small decorative pin on the jacket of her tailored suit, stopping intermittently to make an assortment of moues in the mirror to check her lipstick.

Her makeup did not offset the effect of the deep wrinkles creasing her cheeks and brow; she looked as if she knew firsthand every shoddy trick the world had to offer.

"I won't take a minute," I said, getting my breathing under control. "I want to know when Dutchy showed up at the Sons banquet."

"After the murder. Anything else?"

She was in no mood to be expansive.

"You mean you didn't see him till after Poe was killed?"

I didn't think it possible for her to frown further, but she managed it. An additional cleft appeared between her brows. "I believe," she said with some asperity, "that is what I said. What else did you come to ask?"

"Did Dutchy have a grudge against Wayne Poe?"

She laughed, a short, ugly snort. "Who didn't?"

"What, specifically?"

She clamped her jaw shut. "That's something you will have to ask my husband." She flicked off the light switch. "I have to go. Good-bye."

"Just one thing."

She glanced at her watch. "What *is* it?"

"Does Dutchy own a typewriter?"

"No, but I do."

"May I see it?"

"Why?"

I told her exactly what I needed to see it for. She uttered an exasperated "tch," but walked with brisk heel-clicks down the hall, jerking her head for me to follow.

She opened the door to a dark, dusty workroom. On a table piled with ledger sheets and long technical-looking galleys there was an SCM electric. I took out the note, put it on the table and asked if I could take a sheet of paper. She nodded, looking over my shoulder.

I typed a few letters. It was not the same machine. The ribbon might have been changed, but I doubted that the author of our warning missive would think to alter the keys from pica to elite.

I threw away the comparison sheet and thanked her. She didn't acknowledge it.

I left at the same time she did. I offered to share a cab with her if she was headed uptown, but she declined.

I caught a taxi on Eighth Avenue and told him to leave me off at 85th and West End. During the ride, I mused over the odd circumstance that Isabel Hovis had submitted, albeit impatiently, to my questions without wanting to know why I was asking them.

I tried to let myself in with my key, but it didn't fit. Hilary apparently had the lock changed. I rang and submitted to the Manhattan ritual of peephole scrutiny. Every man's apartment a speakeasy.

Harry let me in. Hilary was at a press luncheon. I went back to my room and stuffed a suitcase with clothes.

"I'll come back for the rest later," I told him, heading for the door.

"Hold it, Gene. Hilary said if you showed up, she had a present for you." He rooted in my old desk and brought out a small manila envelope. It was slightly bulky. I thanked him for it and stuck it in my pocket without opening it in front of him.

Outside, I ripped it open. There were two things in it: my severance paycheck, and a paperback book.

It was an anthology entitled *Feminism: The Essential Historical Writings*. There were several pencil marks opposite page numbers in the table of contents.

My first impulse was to toss it in the corner trash basket. But I changed my mind and stuck it in my back pocket.

I walked over to 85th and Broadway and deposited the check in the bank before grabbing lunch at the Maravilla.

"You did *what*?"

"Tailed 'im."

The Old Man stuck out his chest proudly.

"*Why*? What for?"

"Oh, boy, don't you know? That's what detectives do!"

I counted to ten, then asked him as calmly as I could what good it could possibly do shadowing Phil Faxon after the murder had already been accomplished.

He had no answer, though he tried to improvise one. I waved for silence, went over to a telephone and tried Phil's number. He was in. I made an appointment for later that evening. I wanted to meet him right away, but Faxon insisted we drop by his apartment after ten.

I hung up and turned to the Old Man. "From now on," I said, "we're working together."

"Good idea, boy. You can watch me and learn a few tricks."

This time I counted to twenty.

I wasn't about to return to Hilary's for my gun, so I made sure Butler's was capable of firing, and that he knew how to use it. I don't usually consider a weapon a necessary adjunct to an investigation, but this was different. We'd been threatened twice, and we were about to visit one of the prime suspects.

Arteseros, the desk clerk, gave us a description of the man who'd asked for our room number the night before. It sounded like Phil.

I've never been able to figure out the architectural inception of certain Manhattan houses. In the fifties, there is a showcase theater which does not front any street. To reach it, it's necessary to walk through the hallway of an apartment building and emerge in the backyard where the theater sits in the middle of a brick courtyard.

Faxon's apartment was a similar deal. He lived off a narrow slummy East Village street . . . actually in the Lower East Side, if one ignores the euphemisms of block associations and landlords.

Before I could ring the buzzer, the front door opened. It was Faxon, waiting for us. He was dressed in gray wool slacks, a heavy sweater, and topcoat. I wondered whether we were dealing with a man who'd totally slipped his gears. The temperature was in the eighties. Beads of sweat ran down his thin nose.

"Welcome," he said, smiling, "welcome to the Inner Sanctum." It was, of course, a perfect imitation of the Voice of Raymond from the old radio show.

He escorted us to a coffin-small elevator. We all squeezed uncomfortably, the Old Man's belly taking up the greatest

112

portion of the breathing space. Faxon pushed the sixth-floor button and the door groaned closed.

"Bet you think," Phil said as the elevator crawled slowly upward, "that I gotta know somethin' about that goddamn Heeb's death. Me standin' by the kitchen door an' all, right?"

"Goddamn right, we—" Butler began, but I jabbed an elbow in his gut to shut him up.

"*Do* you know something?" I asked Faxon.

He scratched his straw-dry, gray hair, then wiped his palm against the side of his face, which was covered with stubble and sweat. "Maybe I do. Maybe not."

The door opened. We tumbled out, glad to be able to expand our diaphragms to normal capacity.

"This way, gents," our host said, starting down the hallway toward a door over which a sign glowed: EXIT.

Faxon talked in a mutter that might have been a footnote to himself. "Might tell somethin' you'd want to know."

"What's that?" I prompted.

"That knife they pulled outta Poe. Didn't you never see nothing like it before?"

Butler started to answer, but I nudged him again. The idea is to keep the suspect talking, not supply him with possible answers.

"Why do you ask? Did you recognize the knife, Phil?"

He stopped at the door, opened it, and turning, laid his finger aside his nose and grinned cryptically.

"Trust me," he said. "I know."

He stepped through the door onto the roof. Butler and I followed. The building described a kind of square-cornered C at its top and we were on one of the arms of the letter. Faxon pointed across to the other, separated by a narrow empty gap across which a wooden walkway had been stretched. On the opposite side, a flimsy lean-to glowed with light.

"That's my penthouse," he said with pathetic hyperbole.

"About the knife, Phil?" I asked.

"The knife, yeah," he replied, stepping onto the wood walk. "I know who it belongs to." He gestured to Butler to stand back. "Don't come across till I'm over. This thing wobbles, was only meant for one at a time."

113

It did more than wobble. When Faxon was halfway across, there was an ominous splintering crackle.

"What the holy hell—" he started to say, then changed his mind and began to scream.

The crackle turned into a complicated cracking and the little bridge buckled under him and broke into two hanging fragments. Faxon plunged through and down, down into the darkness, screaming all the way.

There was a muffled thud and a groan, as if from a long way off. Butler rushed over to the edge of the roof and I joined him, peering into the depths below. It was pitch-black, no way of telling whether he'd fallen two stories or ten. We couldn't see Faxon at all. I yelled down to him, but there was no answer.

"Godalmighty!" the Old Man said in a low voice. "We were warned somebody'd get hurt . . ."

I sent him back to the street to phone for help. There was no way to get across the gap to Faxon's apartment. The middle section of the C in which the roof was shaped was blocked by a rise of two additional stories.

I was in the hallway when Detective Irv Katz came puffing along with Butler. A pair of stretcher-bearers brought up the rear. I wondered how they'd all fitted into the tiny elevator.

"Lou sent me along when he heard it was you," said Katz. "Why aren't you out there, watching in case the guy who did it is still in the vicinity?"

"That's exactly why I'm in here," I said. "I'm unarmed."

The elevator opened and another detective ran along the hall and caught up with Katz.

"Okay," the thin, sad-faced policeman told Butler, me, and the hospital attendants, "hold it just a second while Gabe and I check it out."

They pushed open the roof door and carefully walked through, guns ready, flashlights in hand.

A moment later, Katz stuck his face back in. "What the shit are you trying to pull, Gene?"

"Huh? What are you talking about?"

"Come on out here, smartass!"

I stepped onto the roof, the Old Man behind me. The other

detective was shining a powerful light into the abyss. We walked over to the ledge and peered down where the light indicated we should look.

There was no one there. The only things we saw were a couple of mattresses piled on top of one another.

It couldn't have been more than a six-foot drop.

"You shoulda let me play 'Chopsticks' on his teeth!'' the Old Man howled.

I told him to shush. We walked glumly out of the old building. I'd tried to get Katz to let me into Faxon's apartment, but the detective, relenting slightly, admitted someone might have been playing a practical joke on us but still, there was no cause to permit us to break and enter.

I was sure Faxon would be back, too. Further flashlight investigation showed a ladder farther along the shallow brick gulley. There was also a splattered watermelon which must have been responsible for the sickening squelching noise that I'd thought was Phil's body hitting cement. An old trick from radio days, one Faxon would be intimately familiar with.

"Hey, boy, can't we stay awhile till the cops take off? Then we can barrel-ass our way back in!"

"Old Man," I said, "it's my license you're trying to play fast and loose with!"

I didn't like to admit it to myself, but the detective license might be the last thing I had that Hilary might care about.

We tramped into a Brew 'N Burger and ordered a couple of bowls of chili and a pitcher of beer. After Butler drained off his first glass in two consecutive swallows, he grumbled at Faxon's nerve, eluding us in such a ridiculous manner.

"But don't you see?" I asked. "It's positively insane. Why would he stage such a stupid scene? He had to know we'd see down there and spot the mattresses and everything."

"It's simple, boy. He wanted to get away from us."

I shook my head. "There's no point in calling us over and faking a death drop. He could have just refused to see us. Or he could have ducked out between the time I called and he told us

116

to come over. He could have done a lot of things. He might have made us believe he'd been murdered by messing up the apartment, throwing around some red paint, anything. Weakening that bridge—''

I stopped. A new notion occurred to me. I didn't like it one bit.

''What's up, boy?'' Butler asked, setting fire to a twist cigar.

''It just hit me. What if the killer really did loosen the bridge? He could have conked Phil on the head, faked a groan, and dropped the melon, and then spirited him away to murder somewhere else.''

The Old Man's jaw flapped open. ''Y'mean he's maybe stuck in a coal chute, right now?''

''It's a possibility.''

He shuddered. ''Cripes, divorce cases are nothing like this mother! What do we do next?''

''Check out Faxon's favorite haunts. See if he's really missing or playing games.''

''O. K., boy, but I gotta call home first and see if Andy's run the business into the ground yet.''

I didn't comment on how far above the ground it actually was. The Old Man returned a few minutes later, looking annoyed. His brother apparently had been picked up by the police for placing illegal bets on the office phone.

I told Butler to leave a message at The Seymour whenever he got back, then said so long to him as he pulled off in the Packard.

I took a long walk. I had thoughts I needed to be alone with.

Wednesday, I tried to find Phil. He didn't answer his phone or doorbell, so I had to assume he wasn't home. O. J. reluctantly supplied me with a list of places he'd done voice-overs at. I made the rounds of recording studios, but didn't even turn up a mention. He hadn't worked in months.

At last, I tried an agent I once knew. O. J. said Maury Axel occasionally found employment for Phil Faxon. I got Axel on the phone and he informed me that Faxon was supposed to be narrating an army training film that same day.

The tip took me out to Brooklyn and a drafty old warehouse

behind several industrial storage facilities. I wandered in the labyrinth for twenty minutes before tracking down the production unit Phil was hired to work with.

"He called in this morning," the floor manager told me. "Said he was sick. Lucky we've got other material ready to shoot. He's supposed to come in Monday for the stuff we didn't do today."

Monday. Five days away. Plenty of time to escape.

Or hide a body.

I ate alone that evening and retired early. I read in bed for a while before turning off the light. I had to admit Mary Wollstonecraft made some kind of a dent.

There was nothing else I could think to do with Phil Faxon on Thursday, so I swung back to Dutchy. I phoned his apartment and finally got him in. He was cordial enough, told me to come on over, but the joviality sounded strained. Any incursion into Dutchy's private affairs would not get very far, I was only too aware. Knowing his style, I expected he would disarm me with "buff talk" and clam up as soon as I got too personal. . . .

I took a walk down to West 26th. It was only half a buck, but I hadn't yet made up my mind to register for unemployment, so I let my feet take the abuse, instead of my wallet.

Dutchy was sipping mocha java in his living room, a bare chamber except for an elaborate stereo system and a wall of recordings, most of them cinema theme music albums. His dour wife showed me in. "The Rescue of Demetrius" was blasting from the speakers.

Dutchy's thinning hair was ruffled and he was wearing an old satin robe, with grease spots on it, a relic from his old days in the ring. As I entered, he grinned at me, one hand absently flipping his protruding earlobe back and forth.

"Great score, ain't it?" he grinned as I sat down on the picky sofa.

"It's played slower in the picture, as I recall."

He nodded his big head sagely. "Yeah, that's right. But I'll bet you don't know where it first appeared."

I shrugged. "I thought it was part of *The Robe* score."

Dutchy took a big swallow of coffee. I accepted the cup of plain black instant that I told Isabel it was all right to bring me. He waggled his finger at me, lecturing me on his favorite subject movie music.

"Newman is very derivative. Or maybe I should call him

119

self-cannibalizing, that's more accurate. You'll hear the Demetrius action music, note for note, in *The Rains Came.*"

"You mean *The Rains of Ranchipur?*"

"I *mean* what I said—*The Rains Came! Ranchipur* was a remake, for God's sake!"

"Your wife told me you had a reason for wanting Wayne Poe dead."

It was an old trick, the accusing *non sequitur* in the middle of an innocent conversation, but Dutchy didn't even sputter his coffee, the way they always do in movies.

He took a long sip, swallowed, and savored the taste. Then he gestured noncommittally. "Who didn't want that shmuck dead?"

"What was *your* reason?"

"I wrote a script for him last year."

I shouldn't have goggled, but the idea of Dutchy laboring at the typewriter seemed peculiar.

"Oh, yeah," he said, "I know how to spell and all that stuff. I slapped together a show I thought Wayne could do on Broadway."

"And what happened?"

"He sat on it for six goddamn months. Finally I asked the maid to send it back to me. It had brown rings all over it when it came in the mail—like he had nothing better to do but use it as a placemat for his coffee cup. Eventually, I began to hear a couple of the gags from it in his club act."

I didn't ask him whether they'd gotten any laughs.

Dutchy drained the rest of the beverage and set the cup down. "Y'know, as far as motives are concerned, I think you could find one for practically everybody in the Sons, except maybe O. J. Look at Natie, f'rinstance."

"Natie?"

"Well, I shouldn't spread gossip. Never mind. Besides, I understand Natie was right in the middle of the audience when it happened."

"How about you?"

His smile froze. "I beg your pardon?"

"I saw you sneaking upstairs on the night of the banquet . . . long before your wife knew you were there. What were you doing up there on the third floor?''

Dutchy glanced nervously over his shoulder in the direction of the door to the room. He crooked a finger at me and waited till I leaned close to him.

"Get out," he whispered in my ear, "before I punch your face in."

Frank Butler got back Thursday afternoon. He didn't want to talk about his troubles, but finally revealed that his brother was still in the hoosegow and his mother was "minding my business, as usual." The thought of her in his office underwhelmed him. But he perked up when I told him the plan for that evening.

"Hot diggety! We'll take my car! 'Bout time you learned some real detecting, boy!"

Ever since Hilary sold her Opel, I'd relied on taking cabs, or else walking. I would have shadowed Dutchy in a similar fashion, but Butler was too fat to force him to walk and he was afraid of New York cabs, said they were too dangerous.

Earlier, on the phone with O. J., I'd discovered Dutchy was picking up a good chunk of money writing gags for comics. I also learned he had an office in the West 40s which he secured rent-free so long as he did light secretarial work for the owner for part of each day. From personal recollection, as well as the remarks of his wife at the banquet, I knew Dutchy often "worked late." That, added to the way he'd acted that morning, plus his behavior the night of Poe's murder, totaled something that could be proven by watching him carefully for a few days.

I asked the Old Man to stay in the Packard, but he was having walnut withdrawal symptoms and had to duck into a nut shop to get a bag. Naturally, as soon as he left, Dutchy emerged from his office building.

When Butler got back in, I told him he'd lost our quarry.

"Which way'd he go?" He gunned the motor.

"Into the downtown IRT. How are you going to follow him there?"

"Leave it to the Old Man!" He put the car in gear. It lurched

122

forward, just missing a crosstown bus. Butler maneuvered around it and then nosed north into Seventh Avenue.

I yelled. "What the hell are you doing?" I pointed to the sign. "*One way*! The other way!"

"Oh, yeah, I didn't notice," he grinned sheepishly.

But there was no way of getting back, and he had to head up a block, dodging oncoming traffic. The cacophony of automobile horns was louder than Verdi's Hell.

Somehow, we made it without smashing up. He started to turn the car right. The wrong way again.

"Get onto Broadway!" I ordered him. "Left!" Fortunately it was a very short distance.

When we were back in the mainstream of traffic, I wiped my forehead and asked Butler what the hell he'd been trying to do.

"Just wanted to follow the subway line along," he explained. "We can wait at every stop and see if Dutchy gets out."

I closed my eyes. "First of all, you were headed the wrong way. And how in hell are we going to know exactly when he gets a train? He could be ahead of us or behind and we wouldn't be able to tell."

"I didn't think of that, boy," he admitted.

"Look. Do as I tell you. Head south."

I had a strong hunch where Dutchy might get off.

We double-parked in Sheridan Square for five minutes. Then, as I expected, Dutchy emerged and strode directly across the street to the Champagne Cellar.

"Want me to park?" Butler asked. "We can follow him right on in."

"No. We'll wait. I want to see who he comes out with."

It was a long watch. A cop came along and made Butler move the car, but I got out and stood on the curb until he joined me again, this time on foot.

"I parked two blocks over at a meter. How're we gonna follow him if he comes out now?"

"I did some phone work earlier. If O. J.'s right, I'll bet Dutchy goes to the Firing Squad next, and that's just up the street."

"How do you know he'll do that?"

"Because that's where Sandy Sable is scheduled to perform at ten."

Dutchy emerged half an hour later. Sure enough, the diffident comedienne was holding his arm. They walked up Bleecker and turned into an alcove between two buildings. I nodded for Butler to follow with me.

Over the recess, a narrow marquee bore no words, only a picture of Alec Guinness against a wall, blindfolded, cigarette in mouth. It was a still enlarged from the movie *The Captain's Paradise*.

We stumbled through the opening and down two unexpected steps. It was a dark, bullet-gray room, with metal tables, blindfolds for napkins and gunmetal ashtrays. The two waitresses wore lead-hued stockings and matching blouses with the actual noses of two large shells affixed over the breasts. I shuddered to think what Hilary would say if she saw me in there.

Dutchy and Sandy had a ringside table and were watching a young man do card tricks miserably on the raised step that served as a stage. Dutchy had a shot of something tawny in front of him, but Sandy only sipped coke. She was wearing a blue-and-white gingham dress that was deliberately patterned on Judy Garland's garb in *The Wizard of Oz*. Dutchy was in a light brown business suit and theatrical dark glasses, though the place was dimly lit. He smoked a king-size cigarette in a holder and handled it in the affected manner of Von Stroheim.

There were perhaps a half-dozen other drinkers and diners in the place, a meager audience for the magician. Most of them paid him no mind.

He went on too long, as most "talk" variety acts do, and was followed by a dungaree-clad brunette with long braided hair who strummed an autoharp and wailed that her mother wouldn't let her wed at the ripe old age of sixteen. When she was done, the small group of listeners applauded inordinately for her tiny talent.

Sandy was on next. She mounted the single step, curtsied to the group, then saw me in the back and flashed a bright smile and waved. Dutchy turned around, spotted me and Butler, and frowned. Then he gestured for us to join him at the table.

124

"Interesting coincidence," he remarked as we took our seats.

"We just happened—" the Old Man began to lie, but Dutchy motioned for him to be quiet so he could hear his protégée.

For the next twenty-five minutes, I was treated to a verbatim repetition of every gag Sandy tried out on me the afternoon of the banquet at The Lambs. I was fascinated, though, by the difference in her personality from backstage to spotlight. She showed no trace of shyness as she tossed out one-liners. Her blends while we laughed were executed with the deftness of a juggler.

Her act ended with a few clever impersonations. She retired to sparse but vigorous applause. She sat down next to me and, in the flush of excitement which succeeds a successful performance, felt confident enough to pat my hand.

"Lovely of you to come see me, Jim."

"The name's Gene."

"Of course it is!" She smiled. "And just because you couldn't catch me at The Lambs! Isn't that right?" She meant it.

Dutchy interrupted. "I think he came to see me, too, Sandy." The ominous undertone forced her to turn. Her smile changed to an anxious look. She seemed afraid of Dutchy. Her shoulders drooped and some of her poise sloughed off.

"Okay," Dutchy said to me, ignoring Butler, "so now you know."

"Uh-huh. I figured you were headed upstairs to see Sandy that night. It explained why you were so nervous this morning."

"So what are you going to do with the information?" he asked, the hint of a threat in his voice.

"Not a damn thing, Dutchy. Unless I find out that Poe and Sandy were thick, there's no problem. I just wanted to make sure you had a legitimate reason for sneaking around at The Lambs, and also for wanting to keep it quiet."

"What does 'thick' mean?" Sandy asked, sipping her Coca-Cola. "Like making it with each other?"

"That's it, hon," said Dutchy.

She twisted her mouth in distaste. "Imagine wanting to sleep with *him*. Ugh! He was a miserable—" and she added an

125

adjective and noun unique in the annals of vulgarity. But she looked as sweet and vulnerable as before. I wondered where she'd ever heard such an inventive phrase.

Turning to me, she surreptitiously put her hand on my knee and told me Wayne Poe stole some of her best jokes when she was just beginning. She smiled at Dutchy, but maintained her contact on my leg. "That was before you began writing my material, angel . . ."

"*Ah-hah*!" Frank Butler suddenly blurted out. "So you got a motive, too, blondie!"

She looked at him, puzzled.

"What the hell are you talking about, Butler?" Dutchy snapped. "You think Sandy could hurt *anyone*?"

"Well," she said soberly, squeezing my leg "if I did feel like doing away with a rival, it would have certainly been Wayne! He almost cheated me out of a job last—"

"Come on," said Dutchy, rising, "we have to get over to the Improv."

She rose at his command. "I didn't realize it was so late. Gene, would you like to come along?"

Much to Dutchy's annoyance, I accepted.

On the way out, she informed me that she did three or four showcases each night, seven nights a week. I wondered whether Dutchy was supporting her, and if so, how. Most showcases pay the performers nothing.

I also got her to finish her interrupted sentence while Dutchy stood in the street hailing a cab.

"Wayne and I were competing for the same voice-over TV ad," she explained. "He went in for his interview first, and the account executive, when he saw me, tried to suggest all sorts of lewd things. I can imagine what Wayne told him about me!"

"What happened? Who got the job?"

"I did . . . *after* they heard Wayne was dead."

126

We never made it to the Improv in time.

We got into the Packard and Butler slowed to make the turn into Sixth when there was a slight jolt which threw me forward.

"You stupid clown!" Butler yelled out the window. "Who the hell ever taught you how to drive?" He pulled in his head and viciously jabbed the stick into drive.

At the next light, we were bumped again . . . not too hard, but certainly deliberately. Butler howled out the window twice as loud as before.

I turned around. There was a Chevy behind us. The driver wore a floppy hat pulled over his ears. His face was covered by a translucent mask, one of those bizarre contraptions that take on the skin tone of the wearer while unrecognizably altering the features.

"Old Man," I said softly, "pull out, but drive slowly. Stop at the next light and see if he tries it again."

He did as he was told and the car behind us slammed us once more, a little harder than before.

"I'll fix that cruddy bum!" Butler snarled, opening his door.

"NO! STAY IN THE CAR!"

He paid no attention. Uttering a curse of my own, I scrambled out and rounded the car, hugging the side. Butler was nearing the door of the other vehicle when the driver shoved it into reverse gear and zoomed back several feet, paused . . .

"GET ON THE SIDEWALK!" I yelled.

We both hit the curb at the same time. I yanked Butler's arm, pulling him farther back. The other car sped forward, then stopped and went into reverse once more.

"He was probably bumping us so we *would* get out!" I panted.

127

"Izzat him? I'll fix his lights!" I thought it was a figure of speech—until the Old Man shot the glass out of one of our assailant's headlights with his .45.

An immense cloud of white smoke choked us both.

"Damn it, don't you ever *clean* that thing?"

Meanwhile, the masked menace cut his wheels hard and shot forward to make a getaway on Sixth Avenue. Unfortunately, he was too near the Packard and couldn't avoid the door which I'd left wide open when I got out.

There was a metallic rip that was fascinating to hear and afterward, a loud clang. The Chevy kept going.

"What was that noise?" Butler asked suspiciously.

"Your front door." I rounded the car, picked the thing up from the street and showed it to him.

Butler unlocked the trunk, tossed it in, then sourly told me to get in the back seat.

The Chevy was several blocks away by the time he got the car started again, but traffic was sparse and we could still see it. Butler jammed his foot on the accelerator as hard as possible and we roared along, breaking every speed law, crossing red lights.

"It's not worth it!" I told him. "Let him go!" But Butler pretended not to hear me. Or maybe he wasn't pretending. There was a hell of a wind in the car from the hole where the door had been.

The Chevy was stuck at a light. This time, Butler did the bumping, then started to get out, but the light changed, so he slammed the door and we were off once more.

It was up one avenue, across a side street, down another avenue. Our quarry could not shake Butler. I did my best to jot down the other's license number, a New York plate, when we got close enough.

The chase took us to the base of the island where the buildings are tall and the streets incredibly narrow. There our luck ran out. The Chevy shot a red light and Butler tried to do the same. But there was a car coming the other way. The Old Man hit the brakes and I almost landed in the front seat.

Butler leaned on his horn, but the car in the cross street stayed

128

in the middle of the intersection, blocking it. Its door opened and someone got out and approached us.

It was Inspector Lou Betterman.

He let us off fairly lightly. We were treated to fifteen seconds of colorful imprecations and a warning to Butler never to come anywhere near him again. But to me, Lou was reasonably civil, considering the circumstance which brought us together.

"Why don't you and Hilary grow up?" he chided. "I was just talking with her. Both of you want each other, and neither of you knows what to do about it."

"About the only thing I can do, Lou, is to work on this Wayne Poe business and impress the lady."

His eyebrows shot up. "Since when did I ask for any help on it?"

I knew him well enough to understand the implication. He evidently had somebody in mind for the honors.

"Did you tag somebody, Lou?"

"Not yet. Soon."

Which meant there was no chance of getting the name.

Sandy and Dutchy were no longer at the Improv, so we decided to turn in. The doorman eyed the car with surprise, and Butler made me carry in all the six-packs so the garage attendant wouldn't be too tempted by the missing door to assuage his thirst.

At the elevators, the desk clerk hailed us. When we approached, he presented us with a package which he said had just been left for us.

"How long ago?"

"Maybe ten minutes back. A man with gray hair, same one who asked about your room the other night."

I turned and saw Butler unwrapping the box.

"*Don't*!" I snatched it away and held it up to my ear but didn't hear anything.

"Jeez!" said the Old Man, "I never thought of that!"

He never thought of anything.

I summoned a bellhop and told him to bring a bucket of water. Then I made the night clerk clear the lobby, and I rung up Irv Katz at the 24th Precinct. He said he'd rouse the bomb squad right on over, and instructed me what to do till then.

It didn't take them long to get there. Katz was with them and he stood outside with me and Butler.

"This had better not be another gag," the detective warned us.

He had a lot more to say when the squad opened the sodden parcel and found nothing inside but a toy piano with six ten-dollar bills stuffed under its lid.

"I only got one thing to say," Butler replied when I asked him for ideas.

"What?"

He placed his forefinger against his lower lip and flapped it in the conventional childish depiction of lunacy.

"Cut it out!" I growled. "And pass me that bottle."

We were both lying on our beds, too keyed up to go to sleep. He stretched over and let me take a swig of his gin. It was the weirdest-tasting stuff I'd ever tried.

"What the hell's in this, Old Man?"

"Walnut extract."

"Omigod," I murmured, closing my eyes. But he was still there when I opened them—an evil-tempered troll puffing his aromatic twist stogie and guzzling walnut gin.

Butler shook his head. "Too much goddamn pussyfooting," he grumbled. "If we'd worked that crud over, we wouldn't be lying here wondering whether we're gonna find cherry bombs in the john and chicken gizzards in our socks!"

I was almost ready to agree with him on the question of how to interrogate a suspect. Things were getting altogether too screwy. The miniature piano clinched it. There was a rickety bridge in *Swiss Miss*, over which Laurel and Hardy attempt to carry a piano. Aficionados know that the Hal Roach studios edited out of the film a moment when a revolutionary tosses a bomb inside the instrument—a fact which would have motivated the frequent accidental pounding on various piano keys as the boys try to lug the thing across the narrow footpath. Evidently, our assailant knew his Laurel and Hardy intimately, and very possibly figured we did, too. The toy piano practically shouted to us that it *could* have been an explosive device.

But why the money?

The description of the man who delivered the package fit Phil. But I couldn't decide whether he was the actual culprit— or if we were only *supposed* to think so.

Meanwhile, I had a call in to a friend of mine, Leon Sallis, at a state police HQ. I asked him to track down the owner of the license number of the car that battered the Packard.

"Hey, boy," said Butler, "I been thinkin'."

"What about?"

"Sixty bucks'd be a big help fixing my car door. Wanna play me for your half?"

"Play what? We don't have any cards."

He got up and went to a side table which he'd managed to litter with discarded walnut shells. He plucked three of them out of the debris, then fished in his pocket and pulled out a little plastic container. He opened its lid and took out a ball bearing.

I laughed. "You're going to pull the old shell game with *that*?"

"Why not?" he asked, eyes wide. "Works as well as a pea, don't it?"

"Sure, sure, Old Man!" I swung my legs out of bed and examined the metal ball to make sure it was as solid as it looked. "Okay," I nodded, suppressing a grin, "you're on."

I slapped five dollars down on the bed. He did the same.

A moment later, he was holding my five.

In five minutes, he had the entire thirty dollars.

I'd accepted the bet because I knew he couldn't work the classic dodge of slipping the pea out by rolling the shell over it. You can't do it with an unyielding metal sphere.

He started to count his money and I snatched up the shells and examined them. There were tiny bits of metal glued to the inside top of each.

Magnets.

"Okay," I sighed, "give me back my money."

He frowned, as if I were an especially slow-witted child. "C'mon, boy, you know better'n that. I cheated you fair and square!"

Just then the phone rang. It was Leon, my contact in the state police.

132

"Gene, that was a rented car," he said.

"Under what name?"

"Oliver Wheaty."

I sat up. "Give me that again?"

"I *guess* that's how you pronounce it."

"Give me the spelling."

"W-h-e-e-t-e."

I thanked him and hung up.

After a minute, I turned around to tell the Old Man, but he'd sneaked out while I was on the telephone.

First thing Friday morning, I rang up O. J.'s number, but his wife, Della, said he was out of town and wouldn't be back till Monday. I asked where he'd gone, but she couldn't or wouldn't fill me in.

I didn't want to spend three days doing nothing, so Butler and I decided to go question Natie and find out whether Dutchy was right about him having a motive for murdering Poe.

We found him at The Lambs, dressed in a short green tunic and matching cap with a red feather in the band. He was rehearsing something on the third-floor stage with Toby Sanders, who was similarly dressed.

The stage was arranged to look like a bar, and at one end, a dartboard hung on the side of a flat. As we walked in, Toby was pointing something out in the opposite direction for Natie, who obligingly looked away from the dartboard long enough for Toby to stick a dart into the middle of the bull's-eye. Toby then produced a thwacking sound with his mouth and Natie, turning, did an exaggerated double take. Then he took his own dart, aimed it from across the room, and threw it.

Butler and I gawked in amazement. The projectile lodged in the back-feather end of the dart Toby'd planted.

I hailed Natie and he came down the side of the steps, shielding his eyes to see who it was.

"Gene," he called, smiling as usual, "is that you?"

"Yep. What are you two doing? It looks like—"

Natie nodded. "Robin O'Hood, the Irish pub sketch. Toby and I are going to perform it at the Philadelphia convention as a tribute to Black and White."

"How in hell'd you *do* that, boy?" Butler exclaimed, pointing at the darts. "How long'd you have to practice?"

134

Natie laughed. "That's a trick target, for God's sake! You think I can duplicate the original? I borrowed it from Russell over at the Magic Mecca on 53rd."

Butler tromped up the stairs so he could examine the target close up. He was probably wondering whether he should buy one, and if so, how he could use it to swindle me out of some more capital.

"What can I do for you, Gene?" Natie asked. "I've got to get back up there with Toby, I can only spare a minute."

"Dutchy says you had a particular reason for wanting Wayne Poe dead."

He stared at me for a second, then whistled low. "You don't screw around, do you? You go right for the gut."

"You know Frank and I are trying to find out who killed Poe."

"Yeah, but it never occurred to me you'd be sticking it to me." He shook his head, trying to clear it of the giddiness I suppose my question brought on. "It's really a family thing, Gene. I hate to say it's none of your business, but—it isn't."

"Would you rather talk to the police about it?"

I tried not to sound like I was threatening him, but there was no polite way to do it. Natie chewed over it for a while, then, with downturned mouth, gestured for me to join him at the back of the theater.

We sat down in the end seats of the two last rows. I turned my head halfway to catch what he was whispering.

"My sister Renee used to date Wayne. I fixed them up, for Christ's sake! But I'd only been in the Sons about a year, and he was the first celebrity we ran into at a meeting. I was impressed, and she was even more starry-eyed. I mean, she was only twenty-two at the time."

"What happened? He drop her?"

"The son-of-a-bitch knocked her up!" His vehemence had its effect; I had to wipe off my ear.

"Look, Gene," he said unhappily, "is all this really necessary?"

"Maybe not. Nowadays, getting a woman pregnant is not exactly a blood-feud business."

"Yeah," he blurted, "but the crud said he wouldn't support the kid, even if she went to court and stuck him in jail. Instead, Poe provided her with the name of a 'good doctor.' It was in the days before abortion was legal in New York."

I drew some air between my teeth. "Did she go?"

"God, no! She's got *some* brains. Couple of weeks later, as a matter of fact, we read in the paper that the quack Poe named was being disbarred for unsanitary reasons, malpractice, you name it."

"So what happened to the child?"

"She had it, put it up for adoption. We didn't have the money to make a big federal case out of it."

I patted him on the shoulder as I rose and told him not to worry, I wouldn't tell anyone about it.

"I couldn't have killed him, Gene. Not that I wouldn't have enjoyed it. But I was right in the middle of the audience. You can ask half a dozen witnesses."

"Okay. We have to get their names, I suppose, but I'm inclined to believe you. It's too easy to check out."

Natie stood and I moved to the side of the aisle to let him pass, but he stood there looking at his hands, trying to make up his mind about something. Finally, he spoke.

"Gene, I . . . I wasn't going to mention this to anybody. Like I say, I'm glad Poe got it. But it never occurred to me somebody innocent might be tagged for it."

"You know something, then?"

"I saw something."

"What?"

He shrugged. "It doesn't make sense."

I laughed. "What *does* in this nutty case?"

"After Poe fell, you climbed onstage with O. J., remember?"

"Uh-huh."

"You turned and told everybody to keep back and give him air. While your back was turned, I saw O. J. do something."

"What?"

"Take out his handkerchief."

I looked at him like he was crazy.

136

"Are you being *funny*, Natie? Maybe he wanted to wipe his forehead, it was hot. Or maybe he wiped his nose."

He nodded. "He wiped something, all right."

"What?"

"The knife."

Natie went back onstage and continued the rehearsal.

I thought it over for a while, then decided to run over to Grand Central and see O. J.'s wife, Della. The Wheete hat and clothing accessory store is a small fashionable shop just around the corner from the station on Vanderbilt Avenue.

Just as I'd made up my mind, the rehearsal ended. Natie changed to his usual orange T-shirt, an action which quickly ignited an argument between him and the Old Man. Toby wisely ducked out, which left me to be an unwilling moderator on the question of who was more attractive, Mary Tyler Moore or Susan Seaforth, the Old Man's favorite on "Days of Our Lives."

I tried to equivocate by pointing out that both were terrific choices, but the disputants insisted I take sides.

The Old Man grumped at me all the way over to O. J.'s.

But when he recalled what Della looks like, he forgot to be mad any longer.

"Jumping bulldogs," he murmured, "what a broad!"

When we walked in, the honey-blonde was just completing a sale of a skypiece to a young man who plunked down his money without ever seeming to notice the merchandise. She was wearing an orange blouse made of some translucent material and matching slacks, tight enough to delineate without overstating the case.

The customer said something silly as he took the wrapped package. Della giggled as if he'd studied Funny from Mel Brooks.

"Gene," she greeted me after the young man left, "I was just talking about you. I hear you're between gigs."

I nodded. "Hilary let me go."

"She told me on the phone. Not ten minutes ago."

That surprised me. "I thought you hardly knew each other."

Della nodded. "She phoned to talk to O. J., who's still out of town. I asked her something, she asked me a question, and eventually she was talking about her problems. Does that seem strange to you?"

It did. Hilary never opens up to people, least of all a comparative stranger.

"It's not so peculiar," said Della lightly. "I was explaining all the trials and aggravations of being a Sons widow."

Butler punched me in the belt. I apologized for forgetting to introduce him, then rectified the omission. The first thing he did was to proposition her. She laughed as if he were the greatest kidder in the world, simultaneously salvaging her honor and his ego. Then she turned to me and asked the reason for our visit.

I told her I positively had to get in touch with O. J. When she tried to put me off, I gave out with Natie's news about O. J. wiping the knife.

It didn't phase her. "Sounds just like my husband. If you're eating spaghetti, he's liable to reach across and wipe your chin."

"But where is he? Why can't you say?"

She sighed. "He's in Altoona. Our plant had a minor fire and he had to go look over the damage. We don't want the story to get around, or we'll have scared creditors hounding us."

I assured her I wouldn't say a word about it. "One more thing, Della . . . did Wayne Poe ever get fresh with you?"

She laughed, showing a perfect set of teeth. "Of course he did! So what?" She looked over her shoulder. "Don't *do* it, buster . . ."

She smiled when she said it, but there was enough edge for Butler to decide to busy his hands on some neckties on display, rather than where he'd first intended.

"Doesn't O. J. ever get jealous?"

"Of what?" she replied, a teasing mockery in her voice and eyes. "Is there anything he should be jealous about?"

She inhaled as she said it, not by accident, and I did my best to keep my eyes on hers. Ignoring her question, I asked for the phone number of their factory.

"The phones are out, Gene, because of the fire. You might be able to get him at the Nittany Lion in State College. He likes to stay there, even though it's thirty miles away."

"Maybe you'd better give me the address of the plant."

"Sure. I'll write it down for you."

While she scribbled it, I told the Old Man to get ready to go. He had a green beanie in his hand. It had blunted fishhooks stuck all around the crown. He asked me what I thought of it.

I told him, but he bought it, anyway.

"Why should I listen to your taste in hats, boy? You can't even tell the difference between a pretty girl and a *woman*."

He was still ticked off at me for choosing Mary over Susan.

You probably already have it figured, but I was still too hung up with thoughts of Hilary Quayle. I ought to have had part of the answer that Friday, but the pieces didn't start clicking into place until Monday afternoon.

If I hadn't been near the phone to get Hilary's call, it probably would have taken longer.

Here's how it went.

Friday afternoon, Butler had the door to the Packard fixed. We ate dinner at the Shalimar, then took off for Altoona to find O. J. We arrived just before eleven, thanks to Butler's maniacal driving—but O. J. was already gone. We backtracked to the Nittany Lion Inn, but he wasn't there, either. Apparently, while we were speeding across the Keystone Commonwealth, O. J. was already heading in the direction of New York.

In the morning, we dragged ourselves to the Packard and took a little more time getting back to Manhattan. I called the shop right away, only to learn, to my utter disgust, that a new crisis at the plant had forced O. J. to turn right around and drive back to Altoona.

"I say to hell with it!" Butler complained.

Reluctantly, I concurred. We drove another hundred miles to Philadelphia. There, Butler disappeared to sort out family business and I collapsed on his bumpy couch.

I spent most of Saturday sleeping, rousing only to eat a late dinner with the Old Man. On Sunday, I lolled around, reading the book Hilary'd given me most of the morning. I took a walk for lunch—Butler being away—then returned, let myself in with the key he'd provided, and started on the *Times* acrostic.

The phone rang. I picked it up, figuring it was my host.

It was Hilary.

I sat up straight. "I didn't expect to hear from you again."

"Harry said you stopped over for a few things, and you called once. That's all *I* heard."

"Harry takes good messages."

A silence.

I finally broke it. "I've been working on Poe's murder."

"Oh." A dead sound. "For the Sons?"

"Yes."

"I see."

"Weren't you doing the same?"

"Not for the Sons," she said.

After that, a long silence. I thought I could hear her breathe, but I wasn't positive. The tempo matched mine too much to be sure.

"I called," she said at last, "because you had a message."

"From whom?"

"Darrell Hovis."

"That's Dutchy. What did *he* want?"

"He said he didn't know where you were staying, but thought I might be able to reach you. He sounded disturbed."

Another awkward pause.

"Well," I said at last, "you reached me."

"Yes."

And she hung up. As soon as she did, I cursed myself for not mentioning the fact that I was reading the book.

Butler had to arrange bail for his brother Monday morning, so it wasn't till late that afternoon that we returned to Manhattan. I'd made a phone call to Dutchy Sunday evening and arranged a time to meet; Butler got me back into the city with barely enough time for us to meet him at the scheduled hour at The Lambs.

Dutchy looked extremely worried. He wasted little time in getting to the point.

"Listen, boys," he said, "I know you've been digging around this stuff. I want to show you something I found under my door."

He put the envelope on the table without further comment. It was already slit open, of course, so I immediately withdrew the folded piece of bond paper and smoothed it out.

The bold typed letters fairly shouted at me from the page:

IF YOU GO TO PHILADELPHIA,
YOU'LL BE SORRY!

I tapped the note with my forefinger. "What does this mean, the joint convention?"

Dutchy nodded. "I'm supposed to officiate at the main initiation ceremony."

"Initiation ceremony? Since when are there formal membership rites? I never—"

"It's something new Jerry Freundlich and Dutchy worked up," Butler interrupted. "Deep dark secret." He winked at me to emphasize the need of keeping my mouth shut.

I stared at the note for a few seconds. Then, all at once, things started clicking.

"Oh, for God's sake!" I muttered.

I'd spoken softly, but Butler picked up on it right away.

"What's up, boy? What do we—"

"Take it easy," I told him. "We've got a little light detecting ahead, then we're practically all set." I stood and motioned him to do the same. I took the note, folded it, and stuck it in my wallet.

"Hey!" Dutchy barked. "What am I supposed to do?"

"Go to Philadelphia," I suggested. "Have a good time."

Which sage advice almost cost another life.

I called the Maggert-Axel agency, got the number of the film studio in Brooklyn, and checked out Phil. Sure enough, he reported to work that morning, but was already gone by the time I phoned.

Butler wanted to chase on over to his apartment immediately, but I was still worn out from the weekend and couldn't see any particular rush. We had dinner at the Xochitl and turned in. I suggested something cheaper than The Seymour, but the Old Man liked it and insisted he pay for the room.

I figured he owed me for the shell-game swindle, so I let him do so.

First thing next morning we went down to Phil's building. We had a choice. We could ring his bell and take a chance on his getting cute again. We could buzz other buttons until we found somebody who didn't care who was let in. Or we could decide to fiddle around with the lock to the front door.

It was old, easy to open.

In the elevator, Butler took out his revolver and checked the chamber.

"Put that away, damn it! We won't be needing it."

He gave me a fishy look, but did what I told him.

The walkway was repaired and back in place. I tread it lightly, but the Old Man lumbered across like an elephant doing the rhumba.

I crept around to a window and looked in. Phil was snoozing on a sofa bed. I motioned for Butler to stay still, then made a quick circuit to see whether there were any other accesses besides the front door. There weren't.

The lock was a good one, no chance of picking it quickly.

There was no bell. I nodded, and Butler pounded on the door with his fist.

Phil peepholed us, then tried to pretend he wasn't there, but I called out that I'd seen him on the sofa.

"If you don't open up, fine," I said loud enough to be heard past the closed door, "but we're going to stay here all day if we have to."

The Old Man had other ideas. "Open that goddamn door or I'll put my foot through the window!"

Phil let us in.

His "penthouse" was a one-room studio with miniature kitchen and a closet-sized alcove which I presumed was the bath. The sofa bed and a 16-inch TV set took up most of the floor space, while the walls were covered right up to the ceiling with curios, posters, and pennants from the days of radio drama—Captain Midnight decoders, a red lantern, Jack Armstrong pennants, a huge photo blowup of Carlton E. Morse posing with Jack, Doc, and Reggie from the "I Love a Mystery" program, and (Phil's favorite) a gigantic color poster of Orson Welles as The Shadow.

Under the circumstances, there was nothing Phil could say. I sat down on the edge of his bed, and he waited for me to start speaking.

"The notes went too far," I said, shaking my head. "Too heavy-handed, Phil."

"Notes? Whaddaya mean?" He pretended to look puzzled.

"Come off it! You've been running us ragged, you and O. J., trying to scare us away from finding out anything about Poe's death. Why?"

"Aww, hell, boys, we was just havin' some fun . . ."

"FUN!" Butler roared. "Trying to paste us against the sidewalk's *fun*?"

"I wouldn't've run over you," Phil insisted. "Just was trying to shake you up a little."

"And rip the goddamn door off my Packard!"

"That was an accident. Me and O. J. sent you some money for it."

"Sixty lousy bucks!"

Phil shrugged. "O. J. woulda made it more, but he was

pissed that you shot out the headlight of the rented Chevy.''

"What I want to know," I said, "is why you agreed to go along with O. J. on this business. Didn't you think it was kind of peculiar?''

Phil rose and went to the refrigerator, a small unit set into the sink structure. He took out a bottle of tomato juice, poured himself a glass, and offered us some. I accepted and instantly wished I hadn't when I saw the glass he handed me. Butler made a face at the very notion of a nonalcoholic beverage and declined.

"See, O. J. explained that it was a bad thing for the Sons," said Phil, sipping his juice. "I could believe that. None of your business, snoopin' around, interfering with the police and—''

"Come off it, Phil! Stop being a parrot. How much did O. J. pay you?''

The old trouper blushed deeply and stared into his glass. "Enough," he murmured.

"All right," I sighed, "no permanent harm done, so long as I can get on the good sides of Lou Betterman and Irv Katz again. But stay out of it from now on, Phil. You're unwittingly helping a murderer.''

That did a number on him. His watery eyes bulged and his mouth sagged open. "Leapin' lizards, Daddy Warbucks!" he exclaimed in a perfect imitation of Little Orphan Annie. "You don't mean—''

"I GOT IT, I GOT IT, BOY!''

Phil and I both turned to the Old Man in surprise. He was hopping up and down with glee.

"Stop it!" Phil yelled. "You're gonna knock down somethin' valuable!''

"But I got it!" Butler repeated. "I figgered it out!''

I calmed him down. "Okay, we're listening. What have you come up with?''

"I smack Poe in the puss with the cake, he flops down, trying to be funny for a change. O. J. climbs up, pretends to look worried, then when you turn around and tell everybody to cool it, he sneaks out his hanky with the knife inside, and plants it in Poe. Then, when he sees we're on his track, he panics, hires Phil and—how come you're shakin' your head no?''

147

"I'll explain why."

Just then the phone rang. Phil picked it up, said hello to Natie, then listened.

"First of all, Old Man," I lectured, "the angle of the knife would be all wrong for what you're saying. Second, O. J. is the one member of the Sons who liked Poe, he had no motive, not if Della is telling the truth about him not being a jealous man . . ."

"But he wiped off the knife! And how about this crap with threatening notes and fake bombs and—"

"Add it up," I told him. "He was standing by the dais talking to Chuck. Chuck's back was toward the stage, but O. J. was in a direct line with the wings and the kitchen door. He got on the stage first, remember? Then, according to Natie, the first thing he did was wipe the knife. Don't you see what it means?"

Butler shook his head, bewildered.

"It means, Old Man, that O. J. was at the correct angle to see who threw the knife."

The light of intelligence finally flickered in his eyes. He whistled. "You mean O. J. knows *who*?"

"That's what I think. And he's protecting the murderer's identity."

"Why the hell'd he do that?" Butler wondered. "He liked that louse Poe." He squinted at me. "You have a notion now who done it?"

"No. I want to take what we've got to Hilary."

He started to object, but Phil interrupted.

"Gene," he said, "take the phone. Talk to Natie."

I accepted the receiver and listened as the Sons treasurer gave me his news. I hung up and stared.

"What'd he say?" Butler asked.

"Betterman has arrested the last person I would have picked for Poe's murder."

"WHO?!"

"Hal Fawkes."

The idea of our bumbling vice-president accurately hurling a knife was preposterous.

WINDUP AND REWIND:
16mm home movie.

''Why don't you do something to *help* me?!''

Betterman was off till the fifth, and Irv Katz was damned if he'd talk to me. Over Butler's protests, I phoned Hilary, but she was gone for the Independence Day holiday, too, according to Harry. At least, he wasn't with her.

I knew better than to bother Hilary Thursday morning. Promptly at noon, I rang the bell and insisted that she see me. Harry looked dubious, but he went back to her room and rapped on the bedroom door.

Butler and I sat uncomfortably and waited for her to come out. Harry returned and said she didn't want to see me.

"She won't be able to help it," I said, "unless she stays in her room all day. We're not budging."

She appeared ten minutes later. When she saw us, she turned to Harry, one eyebrow arched, and asked why we were still there.

"Because he couldn't help it," I said. "We have to talk to you."

"About what?"

"Wayne Poe's death."

She nodded. "Yes. He definitely is dead. What else did you want to talk about?"

"Who killed him."

"Who did *not* kill him," she replied, smiling frostily. "Who is on first."

"Hilary . . . please! Do you know who did it?"

"I have an idea."

"*Well*?"

"It's only an idea."

"Do you mind telling me?"

151

"Yes. It's none of your business."

For a fleeting second, I thought about turning her over my knee, but then I remembered the one time I'd tried it and ended up on the floor. She used her own knee on me.

"Look, Hilary," I said as patiently as possible, "it's important we talk about it."

"Not to me it isn't."

"What will it take to make you *listen*?" I was becoming exasperated.

Just then the Old Man stood up. "Look, toots, I don't see where me and Gene need your help, but the kid's been mooning about you all over my couch, so tell you what—I'll have you a contest. If you lose, you listen to Gene."

"What kind of contest?" She sounded suspicious. Who could blame her, considering Butler's track record?

He tried to talk her into going to The Lambs to play darts, but she wasn't having any of that, so he ran through a whole encyclopedia of game titles, but Hilary said no to every one.

"If you're really determined to do this," she said at last, "come with me."

She walked back to her bedroom. Butler, mystified, trailed along, and I followed him. Harry wanted to come, too, but she told him to stay by the phones.

She sat down at her desk and pointed to the wall over the bed where there was a large hanging calendar mounted on a square corkboard.

"Target practice. All right?"

Butler readily accepted. I tried to talk him out of it, but when he wouldn't be dissuaded, I insisted on also being given a shot.

Hilary took a small-bore pistol from her drawer. It used BB-sized cartridges and could be expected to do little damage. The corkboard was thick enough to stop the pellets from marring the wall.

I took the weapon from her, steadied my grip, squinted and fired, then handed the gun back to her. My bullet made a neat hole in the lower loop of the "8" that was scheduled to start the following week.

Hilary's blue eyes held mine for a moment. I smiled at her.

Suddenly, she swiveled in her chair and in the same incredibly swift, fluid motion, aimed and fired. Her bullet perforated the identical "8" that I hit.

But her shot went through the dead center of the smaller upper loop.

Hilary returned my smile with more than a little mockery.

"All right, now it's *my* turn!" said the Old Man, drawing his .45. "Stand back and hold your ears."

"NO! DON'T!" Hilary shrieked—a sound I thought her incapable of producing.

I started to warn him not to use his gun, but it was too late. He blasted the calendar off the wall.

"Migod!" I murmured, awestruck. My ears rang with the deafening explosion. Hilary started to cough and I did my best to wave away the dense white smoke cloud.

When it cleared, Hilary went to the corkboard and ruefully examined the hole in it. The plaster behind had not escaped damage, and I wondered what she would say to the super.

Hilary turned, eyes wide and rather wild. She demanded to know what Butler thought he was doing.

"Well, dammitall!" he howled. "I *hit* it, didn't I?"

She stared at him, speechless, her mouth working but unable to frame the proper words. I was afraid she'd either commit mayhem or suffer a multiple heart attack.

And then her eyes met mine. We stared at one another; I tried to ignore the ridiculous side of Butler's action, but I couldn't manage it. Fortunately, it struck her the same way.

When Harry poked his head in to see what the alarming noise might be, he found the two of us laughing hysterically.

Butler eased him out of the room, then left himself, quietly closing the door. As he did, he grimaced grotesquely at me. I think it was supposed to be a wink.

And then Hilary and I were in each other's arms.

She laughed frequently during the early part of my narration, but as I continued, her bursts of mirth grew more sporadic. By the end, she wasn't smiling at all.

"All right, Gene, recall time," she said when I was finished. "We're going to reconstruct it, piece by piece. I want *everything*."

I knew it was going to be a long process. Before we started, I stuck my head into the hall and suggested that Butler might go out for sandwiches while Hilary and I were working. He looked up from his cards and said he would as soon as he and Harry finished the hand.

Poor Harry.

The reconstruction lasted close to two hours, and at one point I had to run through my minutes of the committee meeting where Poe's name was first brought up as an entertainer for the banquet. At the end, Hilary and I both were sweating, in spite of the air conditioning.

"Just one more thing," she said. "Do you still have the two notes?"

"Yep." I removed my wallet from my pocket, took out the folded slips of paper and handed them to Hilary. She smoothed them on the desk top and studied them, side by side.

"One is darker than the other, Gene."

"Yeah, I figure Phil changed his ribbon. It sure needed it."

She shook her head. "No. Come here and look."

I examined the two messages. It was the first time I'd compared them next to each other. "Ouch! I should've caught that. They were typed on different machines."

"Uh-huh. That's what I was afraid of . . . ."

WIPE TO:
Closeup. Lou Betterman's boiled-fish stare.

Shaking his head, he rearranged his considerable weight in the leatherette guest chair in Hilary's office. "If you don't have any new evidence, don't bug me. I've got my man."

"What makes you suspect Hal Fawkes?" she asked.

"Bring me a beer and I'll tell you."

Waving me to keep my place, Butler got up and went back to the kitchen. I was at my old desk, Hilary at hers. Harry, dead drunk from a protracted session with the Old Man, snoozed in my bedroom.

Betterman sighed. He was on his own time and would have liked to go home. If anyone but Hilary had asked, he wouldn't have come.

The policeman accepted a bottle of Grolsch from Butler, poured, took a sip, and sat back. Never a ball of energy, he was evidently mildly distressed at the effort it would take to go over the case. He took another swig of beer, withdrew his pocket notebook, flipped it till he found the page he wanted and looked at us.

"You ever hear of a fellow named Samuel Wittenstein?"

Hilary nodded. Betterman looked surprised and dubious.

"He was a circus and carnival performer," she said. "He billed himself as The Great Witte."

The policeman nodded, extremely impressed. "You know the damnedest things!" he told her.

"It's no coincidence, Lou. I did some research on *The Knifethrower*."

"Aaah." He poured the rest of the bottle into his glass. "Then you recognized the murder weapon."

155

"Yes. The knife that killed Poe looked exactly like the ones thrown at Mae Busch in the old movie."

Betterman nodded. "I didn't see the movie till close to the end of the investigation. I had to work it from the long end around."

"What," I asked, "does *The Knifethrower* have to do with this Great Witte?"

"He was technical adviser to the film," Hilary replied.

"Not only that," Lou added. "He actually throws a knife during the film."

That surprised Hilary. "You mean when the camera stays on both Mae Busch and the knife-thrower? How do you know that?"

"The old guy told me. Billy White."

"At the AGVA home?"

"What made you think to question him?" I asked.

"Because his brother was The Great Witte."

William Wittenstein = Billy White.

Betterman's chain of logic went like this: the knife that killed Wayne Poe once belonged to Sam Wittenstein, but at his death, went to his brother, Billy. Since Hal is Billy's nephew, the policeman assumed he had easy access to his uncle's curios. The programming of *The Knifethrower* at the same time O. J. invited Poe to appear at a Sons banquet must have put it into his mind to do away with the comic with a weapon that was virtually untraceable. Hilary pointed out that it was asking a lot to imagine that Hal would allow the movie to be screened, thus implanting the image of the knife on a hundred persons' retinas, but Betterman wasn't fazed.

"Killers have done stupider things. Besides, was it so dumb? Only a couple people could be expected to get a good look at the knife, and there was no guarantee they'd recognize it. As a matter of fact, it was more likely they wouldn't connect a three-dimensional, color object with a dagger seen in a scratchy black-and-white movie made more than half a century earlier. And Hal, by the way, is supposed to be the only person who owns a print of *The Knifethrower*. Even the Museum of Modern Art doesn't have it."

"And where do you think Hal learned how to throw a knife that well?" Hilary asked.

156

Betterman shrugged. ''Both his uncles had carny experience. He probably learned from them.''

''Lou, Lou,'' Hilary demurred, ''he's the clumsiest klutz on two flat feet.''

''Might be an act. Have any more of this stuff?''

Butler was snoring lustily. I got up and brought Lou another bottle of Grolsch.

''Opportunity, now,'' he said, wiping his lips. ''Hal claims he was in the john at about a quarter of eleven, but that doesn't let him out because Poe was stabbed at ten to. There's no corroboration, either, for his whereabouts. Fawkes claims he heard somebody else come in about then, but doesn't know who it was.''

I reminded Betterman that I'd seen a pair of feet beneath one of the men's room stalls, but that didn't prove anything. Besides, the time factor still had Hal in a bind.

''Gene,'' Hilary said suddenly, ''did you ever have your watch fixed?''

I looked at her oddly, wondering whether she'd decided to join the side of the loonies who'd complicated the case for me. Then I realized the meaning of the question and put both hands to my head in exasperation. I was thoroughly disgusted with myself.

''You gonna let me in on the secret?'' the policeman asked dourly.

''My watch gains time.''

''So? My dog has fleas.''

''Lou,'' I said, ''you fixed the time of murder according to my watch: ten to eleven. But it was probably closer to a quarter to.''

''So?'' He spread his hands wide. ''That makes me no never-mind.''

Hilary tried to explain. ''Fawkes says he was in the john at a quarter before eleven. If that's when Poe was actually knifed—''

''If. *If.* If my mother ate peanuts she'd be an elephant. There's no back-up to where he says he was.''

''But why would he pick the wrong time when he needed an alibi five minutes later?''

''Because he's dumb!'' the officer exclaimed, puffing out his

157

cheeks like a gale on an old sea chart. "He had the means. *I* say he had the opportunity."

"And the motive?" I demanded.

"That's easy. Hal's younger cousin got smashed by a truck a while back. When Billy heard what happened to his nephew, he had a stroke."

I felt a sudden chill. "Was this a young kid? A singer?"

Betterman nodded. "Name of Bryan Harper. And do you know what Wayne Poe pulled on him in Philly just before the kid was killed?"

The only thing that interested Lou in the least was the probability that O. J. saw who hurled the knife.

We tried to get the Sons president on the horn, but he was still in Pennsylvania, near no working telephones. Della said he'd called her from a pay phone to say he'd probably stop off on the way home at the joint SOTD convention in Valley Forge.

"No hurry," Lou yawned, rising. "I've got Fawkes safe and sound. I can talk to Wheete when he gets back."

Hilary tried to argue him into listening to her, but he told her he was going home, that was that. And he left.

"Wake up!" she ordered the Old Man, shaking him.

"Hah? Wazzup?"

"When does the Philadelphia convention begin?"

He blinked at her blearily for a moment, then suddenly shot up out of his chair, eyes filled with panic.

"Holy hog-warts!" he wailed. "Jerry Freundlich'll kill me! I'm supposed to help set up!"

Hilary repeated her question.

"It starts *tomorrow*!"

"All right, cool it!" she ordered him. "Get me the phone book."

I handed it to her. She flipped through it and found the number she wanted.

"Is Dutchy there?" Hilary asked. I picked up the other line and listened in.

Isabel Hovis told Hilary her husband was already en route to Philadelphia.

Hanging up, Hilary told me to pack an overnight bag.

159

"There's nothing else we can do here till O. J. returns. Meanwhile, if we don't get to Valley Forge, there's liable to be another Sons of the Desert murder."

The three of us were in the Packard in less than ten minutes.

"I'm playing a hunch," Hilary admitted as we emerged from the Lincoln Tunnel. "I could be wrong. Though I don't think I am. What *might* happen—"
CUT TO
"They're all over at Valley Forge already," Butler told us, hanging up the phone in the turnpike restaurant. "We'd better get our asses over there pronto!"
CUT TO
"Where the Christ's name you *been*, Frank?" Jerry Freundlich yelled. "You're *supposed* to be the vice-president, remember? You're expected to work!"

We pitched in to get the convention stuff ready for the next day. Hilary didn't mind. The Two Tars includes plenty of women members.

During the evening, Dutchy showed up, looking worried. He called me over.

"I got another one. It scared my wife, she didn't want me to take the chance, but I told her I trust you, Gene."
CUT IN:
Extreme Close-Up of the note.

> WAYNE POE DIED ONSTAGE.
> YOU COULD, TOO . . .
> DON'T GO TO PHILADELPHIA.

"I want a complete rundown of the program," Hilary told Jerry Freundlich. "Especially any activity Dutchy is involved in."

The Two Tars president nodded. "That'd be the initiation ceremony . . ."

CUT TO

Next morning.

"The bus from New York is here!" I said, looking out the window at the parking lot.

The first ones to disembark were Phil Faxon, Natie, Toby, and Della Wheete. Sandy Sable was greeted by Dutchy and the two of them walked off together, talking.

O. J. still hadn't arrived from Altoona.

So:

LAP DISSOLVE

Long Shot. Interior. Evening.

Nearly 150 members of the Sons of the Desert thronged the immense hall, a room brilliant with chandeliers reflecting off a glossily waxed parquet flooring which might have served as a dance floor (maybe it did) or a surface for basketball and tumbling exhibitions.

The decor was a strange mixture of anonymous functionalism and kitschy attempts to be quaint. The walls were festooned with old silver serving trays, hanging beer steins, and one ferocious moose head with a nine-point rack.

Toby and Natie cavorted in the Irish pub sketch, convulsing the audience. It was amazing how the New York tent's treasurer conveyed the wispy wiriness of the late Jack Black, despite his own considerable girth. The pair performed on a low platform with wings and step units on either side to prevent access from the floor. There were no act curtains, but the management had draped the rear wall in bunting of the official club colors, blue and gray.

Butler and I sat on the end seats, left and right, of the front row. Hilary was back by the main door to the room, and she had a whistle around her neck. If she blew it, the Old Man and I were supposed to hop up on the steps where we could see above the heads of the crowd. She would point in the direction of the assailant for us.

There were many things wrong with the plan:

1. There was more than one access to the room.
2. Enough people kept going out to the bar to make it

impossible for Hilary to keep a perfect watch over the main entrance. It would be easy to miss the person we were waiting for.

3. Dutchy rented two spotlights and planned to set them up for the initiation ceremony. He didn't want the effect he'd worked up ruined by the garish room lighting. That meant it would be dark and extremely difficult to see during the most crucial part of the program.

Hilary didn't like it. She'd wanted to call in the local police, but the officers of the Two Tars put their heads together and nixed it. They were worried that the Sons would walk in, see cops, and turn around and leave. Too many people were still extremely shaken up from the New York banquet.

Hilary had brought her revolver, not the little target weapon, and I had one, too. But so did the Old Man.

Another very definite drawback.

The skit ended. Applause.

Two Tars president Jerry Freundlich strode onstage, clapping. He was tall, barrel-chested, had a great unruly shock of brown hair and a nose to rival Everest.

"I'd hoped," he said, "that the president of the parent tent, Mr. O. J. Wheete, might be here for this part of the ceremony, but he called me earlier and said he might be getting in a little late. But, of course, he *will* be here in spirit for the toasts. Will the following persons please join me? Lehman Wilson, Barry Richmond, Natie Barrows."

When they were onstage, Freundlich announced that the Two Tars treasurer, Lehman Wilson, would give the toast to Charley and Mae. Everyone stood up.

A white-haired gentleman with thick glasses and a frail quavering voice spoke into the microphone. "Here's to the sweetest and the sourest of the Laurel and Hardy sidekicks—Mae Busch and Charley Hall!"

"*Hear, hear!*"

Some eight-score glasses were raised in salute.

"Natie Barrows, the parent tent treasurer, will toast Fin."

Natie, still in his costume, lofted his beer.

164

"Here's to his squinty eye!
Here's to his head of skin!
The crusty, irascible guy
Who we all love . . . our FIN!"

"Hear, hear!"
"The toast to Babe will be delivered by a member of the board of the parent tent, a man who was also its treasurer until recently—Mr. Barry Richmond."

Cheers from the New York people, intermixed with wisecracks.

Barry grinned at the audience and adjusted his glasses. Then he pointed in the direction of the most vociferous roisterers and said, "That'll be enough out of you, as the street cleaner said to the horse!"

Good-natured groans.

He turned to Jerry Freundlich and pointed out that he wasn't a mister, but should be addressed as His Excellency. The other looked rather mystified. Then Barry said hello to Natie.

"Nice toast," he remarked. "How much money do you owe Marty Kondak?" It was a well-known fact that our Poet Lariat kept extra rhymed toasts on hand to help out Sons whose muses deserted them.

"The toast to Babe," said Barry. "I quote from John Bunyan. In *Pilgrim's Progress*, there's a phrase that sums up the position Babe often ends up taking. To wit—'Every fat must stand upon his bottom!' TO BABE!"

"Hear, hear!"
We all drank again.

"I was going to take the final toast myself," Jerry Freundlich stated, "but a most important guest just walked in the door, and I believe it is befitting that he handle the toast to Stan. I refer to the Grand Sheik of the Sons of the Desert . . . Mr. Al Kilgore!"

Wild cheering and stamping of feet. Our smiling, saturnine leader walked onto the stage, waving to the crowd. When he reached the microphone, he tugged his necktie out of his vest and twiddled it at the audience.

165

Everyone skritched their heads like Stan Laurel in response and joined hands to sing "We are the Sons of the Desert." Then the Grand Sheik spoke.

"Sorry I'm late, I just got in. Had some work to do till the last minute, and couldn't make the bus." He did a sudden double take. "What the hell is *that* thing?" He pointed to the moose head. Stroking his goatee, he said, "That animal must of been running awful fast to plow into a wall like that!"

Laughter.

"Seriously, I just got here and—what? The toast to Stan? Jeez, I don't have anything prepared." He shrugged, then smiled at the group. "What can I tell ya? Stan was one of the greatest comedy geniuses that ever lived, and . . . well, if it wasn't for him, I guess none of us'd be here tonight. *To Stan*!"

"HEAR, HEAR!"

All tipped their tumblers. Al accepted the glass of beer held out to him by Jerry Freundlich and took a sip. Some of it spilled down his chin. He eyed the glass suspiciously, then laughed.

"This cat gave me a dribble-glass!" He shook a finger at Freundlich. "I'll getcha for that, Lefty!"

"And I'll drink to that!" Jerry said as he took the glass from him. Raising it in honor of the Grand Sheik, the Two Tars prexy took a swallow, deliberately inundating his shirt in the process.

Someone tapped me on the shoulder. Hilary.

"What is it?" I asked, suddenly tense.

"Nothing yet. I checked the registration sheet. Negative. But stay alert, the initiation's next, and they're going to turn out the lights."

"I know."

She hurried over to warn Butler.

There was a short recess and the setting for the skit was struck. Two tables were brought onstage. One held a bowlful of eggs, a large dish of walnuts, a nutcracker, several pairs of latex gloves, and an assortment of uninflated balloons in club colors. The other table had only one object on it, a large square box with a question mark painted on in black pigment.

"And now," said Dutchy Hovis from the stage, "I'm pleased to announce the commencement of the very first official initiation ceremony in the history of the Sons of the Desert!"

166

Dutchy had on a long astrologer's dressing gown, similar to Merlin's in *The Sword in the Stone*.

"Will the Eggs-and-Nuts Maven kindly escort the candidates onto the platform?" Dutchy intoned with exaggerated solemnity.

Jerry Freundlich, now similarly arrayed in floor-length robe and sporting a bright red fez with gold string on top, walked up to the stage, leading the way for four giggling men and women.

When they all stood in a line between Jerry and Dutchy, the first portion of the initiation commenced. It consisted of each candidate stepping to the microphone to pantomime playing a ukelele while doing the hula and singing "Honolulu Baby," a song from the feature film *Sons of the Desert*. Dutchy timed them with a stopwatch, and the trick was to keep it up for thirty consecutive seconds without cracking up, no matter how many distractions the members attempted. Each candidate got three tries.

As soon as the craziness began, the room lights were turned off and the spotlights illuminated the stage. I got up and took a position along the wall, shielding my eyes from the glare.

There was someone standing at a spot opposite me on the other side of the room. I hoped it was Butler.

It wasn't. The lights came up for a moment while a third member of the Two Tars was summoned onstage for the next part of the ceremony. Butler was a little further back and out of the light. The person I'd seen was Sandy Sable. She was fiddling with her purse, rummaging around inside to find something.

The lights went off again and Dutchy stepped to the microphone.

"Each initiate will execute the following steps in sequence. Place a pair of gloves on your hands. Take a paper bag from the Eggs-and-Nuts Maven and fill it with hardboiled eggs and nuts. But first—you have to *shell* the nuts and eggs."

"With gloves on our hands?" one woman asked ingenuously.

"That's right," Dutchy said, "unless you want to use your feet." A burst of laughter.

The ensuing spectacle was ridiculous, but I could only devote

167

part of my attention to it. Nor could I pay much mind to the next ritual, in which the third Celebrant (whom Dutchy called the Balloonatic) distributed the balloons to each candidate and told them to inflate them and tie off the necks without taking off the gloves. Somehow, after much tribulation, they all managed to do so—but as soon as the last balloon was blown up and suspended on the accompanying string, the Balloonatic methodically walked down the line and popped each one with a hat pin.

"And now," said Dutchy, "we come to the final and most symbolic part of our demi-callipygian ritual!"

(Sporadic murmuring: "Demi-*whaa*?")

He leaned in to the microphone. "It means 'half-assed.' "

"Then whyncha say so, boy?" the Old Man called out.

"Now I have already identified the offices of my colleagues," Dutchy continued. "The Balloonatic and the Eggs-and-Nuts Maven. But I have not yet told you *my* title."

Walking to the central table, he lifted the mysterious lid. Beneath it there was a huge, high-mounded whipped-cream pie.

"I," said Dutchy, grinning, "am the Pie Mage."

A ripple of laughter. There might have been more merriment, but many probably were remembering another certain messy bit of pastry.

"Critics have sometimes unfairly criticized the boys as undisciplined slapstick comedians. We of the Sons of the Desert know nothing could be further from the truth. The hallmark of Laurel and Hardy humor is generally controlled slapstick, a madly logical progressive destruction that only gets out of hand toward the very end of certain films. The greatest pie fight in all film comedy, as we all know, was at the climax of Laurel and Hardy's *Battle of the Century*." Dutchy pointed to the pie on the table before him. "In the spirit of controlled slapstick, we of the ritual committee have decided that it would compromise the innate dignity of the Sons . . ." (Laughter) ". . . if we were to treat every candidate for membership to a whipped-cream pie. Therefore, in this final ceremony, we shall select a single representative for the entire group!"

A bowl of white Ping-Pong balls was brought onstage and

168

placed next to the pie. Dutchy showed a single black ball and mixed it in with the others.

"The candidates will be blindfolded, then they will select one ball apiece until someone draws the black ball. That person will be the scapegoat."

That brought quite a few anticipatory chuckles from the audience, as well as a few shouted suggestions as to who would be the best choice to be smashed with glop.

Hilary hurried over to me. "I didn't want to blow the whistle during this, but watch out. I think I saw somebody sneaking in at the back door."

"Tell Butler," I whispered.

"I already did. Get ready."

"I am."

I circled around to the back of the spotlights for a moment to find out if I could see better. As I did, I bumped into someone.

"O. J.! You finally arrived."

"Just a few minutes ago," he said quietly. "Shh. We don't want to disturb anyone."

I hurried quickly back to my observation post. The black ball had just been selected and Jerry Freundlich was helping the victim, one of the young men, get into a plastic rain slicker and hat. Dutchy had the pie in his hand and was waiting at the front of the stage.

From where I stood I could see a little way into the wings. It was dark, but I thought I discerned a shadow detaching itself from the surrounding gloom. Butler was out of my line of vision. I didn't know precisely where Hilary was. It was up to me.

I crept closer, revolver in hand, but still in my jacket so no one would see it and panic.

"Hey," somebody called to my back, "get down! I can't see through you!"

I turned to apologize, then realized it was no time for a gratuitous display of manners. But the split second of inattentiveness was all Dutchy's aggressor needed.

The audience gasped. Dutchy let out a yelp. I whirled, drawing my gun . . .

I couldn't shoot. A figure in black, with a hood covering the entire head, had Dutchy in a stranglehold and was pointing a pistol at his temple. There was no way to get off a shot without felling Dutchy.

I hoped the Old Man knew it.

"I told you not to come here!" a voice snarled in Dutchy's ear, loud enough for everyone to hear. "You bastard! You don't give a damn about the Sons of the Desert! All it means to you is a way to cheat on your wife!"

I could see the finger squeezing the trigger. Maybe I could leap the distance and knock the gun upward? It was a lousy idea, but the only alternative to certain murder. I tensed for the effort—

Suddenly, Butler's voice bellowed from the back of the hall. "DON'T WORRY, DUTCHY! THE OLD MAN'LL SAVE YER ASS!"

"*No*!" Hilary yelled, also from the back of the room.

The sound of a struggle.

"Give me that gun!" Hilary shouted.

"Leggo my arm, damn it! I'll blow a hole in that—"

Hilary said something unintelligible, and then Butler let out a loud yelp of pain.

"GODDAMN BITCH! You coulda broke my SHIN!"

Onstage, the figure in black no longer held Dutchy, but instead, blundered about in the wings, trying to find the way off the platform.

Whirling, I sprinted toward the rear of the room where Hilary and Butler were still fighting. I felt frantically along the wall for the light switch. Everyone was shouting and calling for help, and there was a general air of chaos.

I found the switch and threw it. The sudden glare dazzled my eyes. I blinked to get used to the light, then, seeing Hilary wrestling Butler, clinging to his upraised gun arm, I sped in their direction.

O. J. dashed in front of me, probably with the same notion to assist Hilary. We collided. O. J. skidded on his pants. I sprawled into the back row of chairs. A skinny woman with a martini lurched forward from the impact, dousing her drink all over a bald man. He yelled something vulgar.

170

People started running all over the place. I struggled to my feet, then finally made it to Hilary. I grabbed Butler's arm and helped wrest the .45 from his grip.

But not before it fired.

Fortunately, the bullet went high. It hit the moose head. The thing tottered, then toppled from its perch and plummeted down toward Toby Sanders, who was standing beneath it trying to avoid being trampled.

"TOBY!" I yelled. "HEADS UP!"

He looked up, surprised, just in time to protect himself with his upraised arms. He caught the moose head, but it was too heavy for him to hold long. His arms sagged beneath the great weight, and it settled on his shoulders.

The woman I bumped shrieked. The man she'd spilled the drink on retaliated by pouring his beer down her bodice. She demanded that her escort defend her, but he was doubled over with laughter. Snatching away his drink, she poured half of it over him and tossed the residue at her antagonist. It missed and doused a big matron in purple.

Pushing me to one side, Hilary started for the front of the auditorium.

"Gimme that gun!" Butler howled, chasing her.

She dodged Toby, but the Old Man piled into the blindly staggering young man. The pair went down, legs flailing on the slippery floor: two men and a moose head.

"*Gene!*" Hilary called above the tumult. "*This way!*"

Trying to avoid the pileup, I slammed into O. J. coming from the other direction. He tottered past and ended up tangled together with Butler, Toby, and the moose. The latter somehow managed to transfer itself to the Old Man's shoulders.

I dashed past the back row of the audience, noticing as I hurried by that the purple matron was taking her revenge by getting even with her enemy's husband, ripping his pants off.

Hilary met me at the front of the stage, face flushed, eyes dancing. She gave me a quick hug, then pointed to the other side of the platform.

"Quick! She ran out the back door!"

We raced to it, flung it open, plunged through. It gave access to a long corridor where the rest rooms were located. Halfway down the hall, a black object lay discarded on the floor.

The hood.

The woman in black was in the corridor and had almost attained the far end. But just then, the door to the women's rest room opened and Sandy Sable walked out.

The woman in black shrieked. Sandy stopped, blinked, then shrank away from the other, but Isabel Hovis leaped and buried her fingers into her rival's blonde hair.

It came off in her hands.

Sandy squealed. She flailed her arms wildly until she gained a few inches of clearance, then started to gallop in our direction.

Isabel, wild-eyed, forgetting her need to escape, headed after Sandy, her fingers clawing the air in front of her as if she already had the comedienne in her clutches.

The corridor was too narrow. There was no way to fire at Isabel, Sandy was in the way. She kept coming straight at us. Neither Hilary nor I could get out of her way fast enough.

We all stumbled backward, out the door into the main hall again. I caught Hilary's arm and stopped her from landing on her fanny. Sandy hugged me tight and yanked me around so I was between her and Isabel.

"Nice to see you, Gene," Sandy panted, releasing me into Isabel's claws. The younger woman scooted back into the hall.

"OUCH!" I grabbed the woman round her waist and lifted her so she couldn't reach my eyes with her nails.

"Put me down!" she ordered, placing her gun at my temple.

I set her on the floor and backed up. She gestured to Hilary.

"Get over there with him!"

Hilary stood next to me. She spoke in a low voice.

"Gene, did you ever see a weapon like that?"

I shook my head. The barrel was too long. The balance would be impossible.

"All right!" Isabel barked, her dark eyes pinioning us like hurled daggers. "Turn and walk. Slowly."

Rounding the platform, we encountered total madness. Nearly 150 members of the Sons were embroiled in a colossal brannigan. Drinks were being thrown all over the room. Pants were being ripped, jackets and dresses torn. One angry couple was busily engaged in a program of shin kicking and hair pulling.

In the midst of it, the Old Man wobbled dizzily around, moose head still in place. O. J. clung to his jacket to stop him from colliding with anybody else, but the floor was too slick and Butler pulled O. J. along as he lumbered about in his elephantine way.

On the platform, Dutchy, standing next to the pie, shook his head in near-terminal astonishment. He flinched when he saw his wife.

Isabel jerked the gun in the direction of the stage and made us climb onto it.

"Take his arms, you two!" she yelled, partly to be heard above the din.

We did what we were told.

"How did you know?" she shouted.

"You were the only person who saw the original threatening note," Hilary said. "When Gene was examining your typewriter, he told you all about it. Very opportunistic."

The other nodded. Then she waved the peculiar pistol and made us bend Dutchy over so his face was right above the pie. She aimed the gun at the top of his forehead.

"You think I didn't know what you and that slut were doing?" she sneered.

"Baby," Dutchy whined, "you're not gonna—"

"SHUT UP!" He did. "I told you to stay away from here, but you *had* to hop in her pants again, didn't you? Now I'm going to give you what's coming to you!"

And she smooshed his puss smack into the pie.

He came up sputtering, startled. The first thing he saw when he wiped the white from his eyes was the barrel of the pistol aiming dead center at the middle of his forehead.

She pulled the trigger.

Dutchy screamed.

The front of the gun flew outward, then quivered to a stop. A gaudy red flag unfurled, dropped into place from the interior of the weapon's long barrel.

The scarlet cloth said BANG!

We gaped at the thing. And gaped.

Then, all at once, Hilary and I began to giggle and guffaw so hard we nearly fell down.

Hilary finally brought herself under control long enough to fling her arms around Isabel Hovis and give her a bear hug.

"Oh, right on, sister!" Hilary said, shaking with laughter. *"Right on!"*

Betterman scratched at the scraggly growth he called a mustache and glowered at O. J.

"Before I decide to release Hal Fawkes," he grumbled, "suppose you tell me how you can back up what you're telling me."

Hilary interrupted. "You'll get corroboration if you'll come with us."

"Yeah, yeah. But first, suppose Wheete explains why he kept this all to himself so long."

The Sons of the Desert president gazed down at his carefully manicured fingers and murmured, "I wanted to avoid a scandal."

"For your organization?"

"Partly. But really more as a favor to Billy."

The policeman sighed. "All right. I guess we'd better go talk to the old geezer."

Frank Butler was still in Philadelphia helping with the regional convention, so there were only four of us in the police car. Betterman drove, with O. J. sitting next to him. Hilary and I shared the back seat.

It was a sunny summer afternoon and the AGVA home looked green and peaceful. The inspector had called on ahead, so it took only a minute to clear with the front desk and be shown to Billy White's room.

The old man looked a lot better than the last time I'd seen him. His cheeks were freshly shaven because he knew guests were coming, and his color was back. The strands of white hair (what there were) had been carefully combed across his bald head, and he'd been helped to dress in jacket and tie for the occasion, even though the weather was hot.

"He insisted on it," the nurse told us.

"A little style is all I've got left," he wheezed. His jaw was still slack from the stroke and we had to listen very carefully to understand him.

He turned to O. J. "So you tattle-taled after all, Oliver?"

"No, no." O. J. shook his head. "This lady figured out what happened, and I had no choice, Billy."

White turned his gaze on Hilary. "Not bad! Come over and make an old buzzard happy."

Hilary went to his wheelchair and knelt beside it.

"Your brother Sam was the adviser on the Irish pub sketch, wasn't he?" she guessed.

He nodded, patting her hand. "Clever. We never told anybody. How'd you know?"

"I learned he did the hardest work in *The Knifethrower*.

176

Then when I saw that incredible shot in the TV kinescope—"

The invalid laughed, a frail ghost of humor. "When I stick the dart into the board while Jackie's back is turned, and then he takes his shot as Robin O'Hood and lands the damn thing right in the tail of my dart! We made quite a splash on the tube with that number."

"I couldn't believe it when I saw it," said Hilary. "The camera didn't move . . . it was done in *one* shot."

White leaned his head over conspiratorially and spoke softly to Hilary, but we all could hear. "Let you in on the secret, angel. That was one of the first taped TV scenes they ever made. Jackie took lessons from my brother, and Sammy wanted to do the shot, but Jackie insisted on doing it himself. He got so he could make it maybe two times out of twenty. We just kept filming it till it happened."

Hilary turned to include the rest of us. "That was the scene that made me suspect Jack Black right away. After I checked into the background of *The Knifethrower*, I was even surer. But by then, he was dead and I didn't see any reason to smear his name."

"*They* did!" White accused.

"Who?"

"Some of those buttinskys down at the Sons of the Desert. O. J. told me about it. I made him promise he'd throw them off the trail. I didn't want Jackie's name and memory destroyed just for doing what he knew was right!"

"Why *did* he do it?" she asked. "As a favor to you?"

"That was mainly it," White agreed. "He knew why I had my stroke . . . because of what that no-good louse Poe did to my nephew Bryan." His eyes strayed to the inspector's, and the old man suddenly hunched over, looking exceedingly crafty. "Understand, *I* didn't know anything about it at the time. Jackie talked to O. J. one night while the Sons was having a committee meeting, and from what I've heard later, he found out that Poe was going to be on the banquet program. So Jackie thought it over and decided to borrow one of my late brother's knives without me knowing about it."

Betterman rose. "Revenge for a friend, eh? *I* should have pals like that."

177

Billy White shook his head. "I said that was mainly it. But there was another reason, young man."

Betterman spread his hands. "So? Give with it."

"No. You wouldn't believe it. You'd think it was an old coot thinking out of his depth."

Hilary squeezed his hand. "I'll bet I can guess, Mr. White."

He smiled at her. "I'll bet you *can*," he said, eyebrows raised expectantly.

"Your partner was making a parting gesture to the art of comedy."

"That's it! That's it!"

Betterman looked skeptical.

"Lou," she said, "you didn't see Black the night of the banquet. He pointedly ignored Poe. And the toast he delivered was more like a prayer to Aristophanes."

I remembered Jack Black berating O. J. in the car for profaning the comedic tradition by putting Wayne Poe on the banquet program.

"Nobody kills for the sake of a few jokes!" Betterman protested.

"Young man!" Billy White said sharply. "You are talking to a man who has spent most of his life trying to make people laugh! My partner was the same . . . ninety years in the business. Just because he was retired didn't mean he'd lost the calling. Even here among the patients he did his best to lighten other's sorrows. My God, man, he was past ninety, I say! Why *not* kill Poe, that blot on the profession? What was there to lose?"

The old man struggled to rise. Hilary helped him by supporting most of his weight. He raised a hand in a commanding gesture.

"Let me tell you, youngster, there is nothing nobler than making one's fellow man laugh at the misfortunes of this tragic business called life. There's an ancient legend that a departed spirit entering the underworld must answer two questions. The first, 'Did you find joy?' is not important. But when they ask the second, '*Did you bring joy?*' the answer had best be a resounding YES or the offender will be fed to the two-headed reptiles.

"Inspector," he wheezed, the burst of energy dissipated, "if

I enter Hades tonight, I expect I'll find my partner Jackie entertaining the whole infernal crew with dirty jokes about damnation!''

Hilary helped him sit back down in his wheelchair. He breathed shallowly for a moment, then gave us all a wink and a wicked smile.

''And I'll bet a month's supply of Kaopectate that right this minute Wayne Poe is trying to save his ass from the crocogators!''

In hopes of keeping the corruption, featherbedding and expense-padding to a minimum, new officers will be elected periodically. The Archivist must keep accurate and up-to-date records of railroad timetables so the old slate may be retired unharmed.
—from *The Sons of the Desert Guidelines to Decorous Behaviour (by-laws)*

O. J. tried to show his gratitude to Hilary by making her an honorary Daughter of the Desert, but she refused the token gesture, so he suggested she take on his firm as a client and she agreed with pleasure. It helps fill part of the financial vacuum created by the loss of the Trim-Tram account.

Hilary and I made a deal. It was my giving up either the Sons or dates with Penny Saxon and Pat Lowe. I decided to stick with the organization, partly because if I'm elected secretary next year, I'm going to try to help change the tent's policy toward women members. Admittedly, it's a task a little less appealing than chewing on razor blades, but I keep remembering the look on Hilary's face when she first found out. The way I figure it, any rule that unnecessarily brings unhappiness to even one other human being ought to be dispensed with.

On the debit side of the ledger, Harry Whelan still has my room. And my job.

Hilary says she's embarrassed, that she only hired him temporarily till he finds work. Giving him my room was an act of charity, because he was so broke he couldn't even afford the Y.

"As soon as he gets cast in another show, or is hired for an industrial, he moves out," she says. Only the way the theater business is, it could be forever before he lands another part, and meanwhile, I have an uncharitable suspicion that Harry is

180

currently not pursuing his career quite so zealousy as he used to . . .

In the interim, I've been commuting back and forth from Philadelphia, where I'm earning some bread attempting to put the Djinn Investigations files in some kind of order. If I succeed, I may tackle the Augean stables next.

This business with Harry really has me bugged. There's nothing much I can do about it, though. Except maybe call Sandy Sable for a few dates. After all, *her* name was not mentioned in my pact with Hilary.

The other day, I asked Frank Butler what he thought about it all. He shrugged and puffed his twist stogie for a minute or two, then gestured with it at me.

"I'm reminded of a couple of things somebody said once, boy. Bacon, I think it was. The first goes, 'It's better to have loved and lost than not to have lost at all—' "

"And the second, Old Man?"

" *'All's well that ends.'* Now pass me the goddamned walnuts . . ."